To my family

And all our Lao friends:
those who escaped and those who remained
behind

CONTENTS

An Open Letter *1*

1. Day One—A Day of Horror *3*

2. Day Two—An Arrest *7*

3. Indoctrination *14*

4. Spy *17*

5. Cloak-and-Dagger Stuff *22*

6. The Package *25*

7. Sabotage *28*

8. Nongkhai *35*

9. The Lee House *41*

10. Stakeout *49*

11. Handover *58*

12. A Funeral *62*

13. A Plea for Help *64*

14. Inscrutable *73*

15. The Plot Thickens *79*

16. Prisoners *86*

17. A Bribe *93*

18. Kidnapped *100*

19. Panic *103*

20. Police Rescue *108*

21. The Chinese and French Connections *111*

22. Doctor Lian *119*

23. Trapped *122*

24. Anna and the Marines *128*

25. At Souphanouvong's Pleasure *138*

26. Waiting *144*

27. Skyfighters *147*

28. No Special Privileges *153*

29. Reconnaissance *156*

30. Joining Forces *164*

31. The Raid *169*

32. The Final Crossing *175*

33. A Letter from Harry to His Friend Nat *179*

Glossary *182*

LAOS and MEKONG RIVER

CHINA

MYANMAR

Hanoi

Mekong River

Gulf of
Tonkin

Vientiane

Nong
Khai

Udon Thani

THAILAND

LAOS

VIETNAM

Bangkok

Pattaya

CAMBODIA

Mekong River

Phnom
Penh

Ho Chi
Minh City

Gulf of
Thailand

THE PORTERS' VIENTIANE

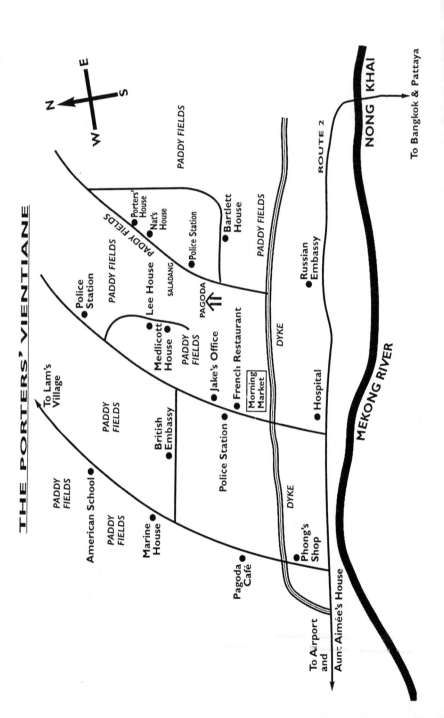

An Open Letter from Harry Porter

Hi:

My name is Harry Porter. In 1975, my family and I were living in Laos, which is a small country squeezed between Thailand, Burma, Vietnam, China and Cambodia. Laos was a kingdom in the centre of the communist struggle, and while the Americans were helping the Lao fight the communist Pathet Lao, the Vietnamese were helping the Pathet Lao.

Laos is a land of mountains, thick tropical forests and rich farmlands. The Lao people farm the lowlands, and the Mao raise opium in the mountains.

We were there because my Dad was a technical expert advising the Lao government. My sister Anna and I went to the American School. She was fifteen and I was twelve. We also had a black labrador dog, Beauty, and twenty rabbits.

My sister and I get on pretty well. Probably because we move around a lot—so we sort of rely on each other. When we discussed about telling this story, we thought we'd do it just from our point of view. Then Anna pointed out that Mum and Dad had had their share of it all, and it was only fair that they should tell their part, and then other people had to tell their bits as well.

So this is our story of what happened to us when the king was overthrown in May 1975 and the premier, Prince Souvanna Phouma, was replaced by his communist brother, Souphanouvong, the "Red Prince," and the Land of a Million Elephants became the Lao People's Democratic Republic.

1

Day One—A Day of Horror

The night sky was filled with red and orange flames. Rockets shot upwards with a whooshing sound, as if leaping to reach the stars; but the stars were hidden behind thick smoke. The air smelt of gunpowder and burning, and the usually quiet night was filled with the boom-boom of explosions and the ratatatat of machine guns.

Harry Porter ran into the house, calling his family to come and see the fireworks. His parents, Meg and Jake, and older sister Anna hurried out to join the group of neighbours standing in the lane. They stood in stunned silence as they watched the centre of their neighbourhood, Saladang, just a five-minute walk away, burn to the ground.

Suddenly a bicycle materialized from out of the smoke and slithered to a stop beside them. It was Nat, Harry's American friend, who lived next door. His face was streaked with soot. Nat leaned over the seat of his bike, coughing and spitting the smoke from his lungs as he tried to catch his breath. It took a few minutes, before he was able to stand up and explain, "Someone threw a Molotov cocktail through the police station window and all the explosives stored there blew up."

There was a shocked gasp from everyone, and then they all began talking at once. Jake asked if there was anything they could do. No, those who survived had been taken to the hospital and the village had been sealed off. It would take days before the fire was completely out.

The fire was the conclusion of the most horrifying day Anna and Harry had ever experienced. They'd been woken very early in the morning by Nat. He'd had alarming news. The communist forces had taken over the whole city in the night. The American compound had been seized, and everyone inside was being held prisoner until they could be evacuated. In the meantime, the marines were barricaded inside the USAID offices destroying files.

To begin with, Harry thought Nat was joking. How could it be true? They'd heard nothing. Everything seemed normal. The morning mist hung a few feet from the ground among the houses, and all was quiet and serene. There were the usual morning sounds—a cock crowing, the swish of water from a rain barrel as someone washed their face and filled a pot to put on a charcoal stove for tea.

"Are you sure?" Harry asked. Nat nodded vigorously, of course he was sure. His dad was with the CIA and he'd been up all night on his radio.

Nat joined Harry's family at the table for a second breakfast. Between mouthfuls, he told them his mum was already packing, and his dad said that once the rescue planes came in, probably tomorrow if they were allowed to land, they'd all be flying home to the States.

"Everyone's going?" asked Harry.

"Sure, there'll be just a handful left at the American embassy."

Harry turned to his father, "Will we be going home too, Dad?"

Harry's father Jake was an adviser to the Laotian government.

"No, Harry," said Jake. "We Canadians are apolitical, and we'll just carry on as usual, the best we can."

"But, Dad, it will be awful if all our friends have gone, and what about school?"

This was a hard blow for Anna and Harry as there was no more school, although there was a whole month to go before the end of the year. Worst of all, they couldn't even say goodbye to their friends before they were evacuated.

The whole neighbourhood was terribly quiet. The only news that came was via Nat's dad's radio. Harry went over to help Nat seal packing boxes with tape, while Anna and her mother prepared food for a farewell supper for their American neighbours. They had the meal early, as everyone was tired after a long tense day.

It was a sad evening. Not only were they saying goodbye to friends, but also this day marked the end of the king's reign and the start of uncertainty and fear under the communists. Many people loyal to the king had fled across the Mekong River to Thailand, before they could be arrested for re-education. The borders were closed, food was already in short supply, and suddenly everyone became suspicious of everyone else.

In the night, Harry was woken by the sound of trucks passing along the unpaved road. Shots were fired, a scream rang out and then, with a grating of gears, the convoy of trucks moved on. The arrests had already begun.

Harry sat up in bed, straining to hear. But all was quiet, except for the dog, Beauty, downstairs. Harry could hear her scratching, then the click of her claws on the floor as she crossed the room to drink from the goldfish pond under the stairs. Then she lay down with a thump and a loud sigh. Harry listened for a while longer and finally fell asleep.

2

Day Two—An Arrest

As dawn gently broke, smoke rose into the air from one or two of the stilted houses, indicating breakfast was being prepared. A dog barked close by, and the wat gong boomed loudly from among the trees.

Harry stood at his bedroom window watching Lian wheel her bicycle to the gate, her feet swishing softly in the damp grass. He crossed his fingers and made a wish that she'd have no problems on her way home. Lian came daily to help his mother in the house, and yesterday she'd been unable to return home because of the curfew. He quickly made a second wish that she'd find her family safe—they must be worried sick about her, as it had been impossible to send a message without a phone.

Harry watched her until she was out of sight. Then an old man passed the gate with his pink water buffalo. The orange-robed monks from the wat followed in single file, carrying their begging bowls. A Lao couple, the Porters' neighbours, were patiently waiting for the monks at the side of the road. The man stood with his head bent, and his wife was on her knees in the dust, averting her eyes. The monks silently accepted the rice from her. The smallest monk at the end of the line, surely no older than seven, received the final scrapping.

Harry crept down the stairs, not wanting to disturb the rest of his family, as they'd all been exhausted the night before. Beauty lazily stretched and ambled after him into the kitchen.

He threw open the shutters and the door, and Tee came in yawning, a large grin on his round face. Tee was the gardener. He and his wife, Somphong, lived in a small house built into the garden wall.

Harry opened the fridge and the three of them peered in, hungry for breakfast. Harry pulled out a crusty loaf and cut off three large hunks, one for each of them. Tee filled the kettle for tea, and Harry poured himself a glass of milk from the jug his mother had prepared the night before. There was no milk available in Laos, so they bought large cans of powdered milk whenever they crossed the river into Thailand.

Harry wandered out into the garden munching, bread in one hand and his glass in the other. Beauty followed.

The garden was surrounded on three sides by a high mellow-red brick wall and a six-foot-high metal gate, which was kept locked at all times to keep intruders out and Beauty in. Beauty was a large black Labrador, and several Chinese had offered American dollars for her. Black dog was believed by the Chinese to be particularly succulent and delicious, and the Porters shuddered at the thought of their beloved Beauty being eaten.

The garden was pretty wild by Canadian standards, but the fruit trees produced good crops of banana, papaya, mango and coconut. The lawns were green and all the plants and flowers were enormous compared to those at home.

At this early hour, everything was delicately speckled with dew. As Harry approached the hutch, the rabbits poked their quivering noses through the slats, expectant for breakfast, and the next-door pigs snuffled noisily under the dividing fence.

More than twenty-four hours had passed since Nat first came over the wall, and now he sat astride it in order to say a last goodbye.

"We're off to the airport, although we'll probably be there all day. There are already major problems—they're demanding money to allow us to leave!"

"I'll really miss you, Nat," said Harry. "So long. Perhaps when I'm back home in Canada, you could come and visit."

"Sure, see you!"

*

Harry didn't have time to miss Nat's company, as he had to accompany his mother to the morning market to see what she could add to their store cupboard.

The road through the village had been opened, and they drove slowly between the blackened remains of the wooden houses. The ruins were still smouldering here and there, and painfully thin-looking "pie" dogs were rooting for anything that might be edible.

Once on the narrow main road, which was built on a dyke between paddy fields, the going was slow as they had to inch their way through a jumble of samlows, buffalo, bicycles and pedestrians. However, there were no road blocks.

The market was back to normal. Small stalls, shaded by
large umbrellas, crowded around a central building. A group
of barefooted boys rushed forward to grab their baskets.
Anna and Harry watched their mother stride purposefully
into the meat market, followed by two of the boys carrying
her baskets. They hated going into the huge hall with its
rows of stone slabs where the meat sellers sat, surrounded
by their displays of meat. Harry found it disgusting. It made
him want to throw up. Dogs snuffled under the tables, and
beggars and porters loitered, spitting betel juice in red
streams onto the dirty floor as they watched the housewives
poking the meat and bargaining with the good-natured, smiling country women.

Harry also had things to do. He plunged into the dark
maze of covered stalls, greeting people as he hurried by, and
went to inspect a case of knives and chat with the merchant.
He had his eye on one particular knife. He enjoyed the battle
of wits they'd been waging for several weeks, as he slowly
bargained down the price. He realized that perhaps he'd be
able to get it for a really good price when the man casually
mentioned to him that he might return to Thailand. Then
Harry felt badly, as he knew his mum would say he was
taking advantage. Anyway he'd not brought his money with
him, so with a rueful smile, he said he'd be back in a few
days and asked whether the stall would still be there.

"Of course," smiled the merchant, laughing at the earnest
young "felang." "I'm still thinking about it, and I will have
to choose an auspicious day to move my business."

Harry caught up with his mother and sister at a dry goods
stall where they were purchasing soap, washing powder and

sugar, just in case these items should vanish from the market. His mother sent Harry to look for candles and matches, two other "necessities" for the house, since the electric power often failed.

The next stop was the stall of two pretty French-speaking sisters from whom his mother always bought the vegetables. They smiled in greeting, "Bonjour, Madame, il n'y a pas grande chose aujourd'hui," they said sadly. "La frontière est encore fermée."

Still there were some carrots, a water melon, eggs and potatoes. Song, a large boy with a big grin and a shaved head, carried the meat and soap powder. A small boy called Mud, in patched trousers and an old baseball cap, struggled with the water melon, Anna had the eggs and sugar, and Harry carried the vegetables, candles and matches. They followed Meg to the car where they were instantly surrounded by a crowd of beggars and small children. Song yelled at the children, who quickly dispersed, and Meg gave a couple of the beggars some change before supervising the loading of the car and paying off the porters.

"One more stop," she said, with a sigh. "We'd better see if we can buy a bottle of gas." They cooked with bottled gas. But it was already too late. The gas seller shook his head, he had no bottles left, and he doubted whether there'd be any for months. He was going back to his village for some time, it wasn't safe in Vientiane any more. He'd heard in the market that a Pathet Lao patrol was jumped in the night and their throats slit.

Tee met them at the gate. His face was sombre and he stated brusquely, "Lian back!"

"Already?" How could she be back so soon? At that moment, Lian came running from the kitchen, tears pouring down her face, and with her came three tiny girls, two of them clinging to the back of her skirt.

"Lian, what is it?"

"Oh Madame, my husband was taken away in the night!" Lian sobbed.

3

Indoctrination

As the nearest Canadian Embassy was in Bangkok, Thailand, the British Embassy in Vientianne looked after the handful of Canadians if a local emergency arose. However, sometimes Jake still had to go to the embassy in Bangkok.

"I've been called to Bangkok tomorrow," Jake said to his wife Meg. "I'll only be away one night, so I thought Anna and Harry could come along."

Meg said that was alright with her.

"Great idea, Dad," Harry said. "Sure we'll come, won't we Anna?"

"Yes. Thanks, Dad." Anna would have gone anywhere, done anything. All her friends had been evacuated and she was dismayed at the thought of a long, long summer without friends her own age.

The family were sitting on the verandah before supper. All was deceptively tranquil, and there was just an occasional rustle, as the neighbours' hens settled on their perches beneath the house for the night.

It was amazing how life could change so suddenly. They'd all done their best to help Lian, but were unable to bring her husband back. Tonight, Lian and her children, and Tee and his wife Somphong had all gone to the wat for a neighbourhood meeting. It made Harry feel left out different—a real *felang*. He hated it when the local children yelled that word at him, but tonight he was glad to be a foreigner. His Dad said the government was very clever to involve the monks, because everyone revered the monks and would follow their lead.

Meg broke into his daydreaming, "Come on, Harry, suppertime. I want to have everything cleared away before Lian and the others are back. They're bound to be upset."

They sat down at the table to eat cold meat, salad and a long stick of French bread.

"Cold soup," said Meg, ladling it out of a large white tureen and passing the plates around.

"Cold soup? Ugh!" said Harry.

"It's good, taste it. It's mint and cucumber, two things we grow ourselves, but the cream came out of a can from France."

Harry tasted it cautiously. His mother was right, it was good. Once the meal was finished, they all helped clear the table and wash and dry the dishes. Beauty had devoured the scraps in one large gulp. Harry was putting away the last glass in the cupboard when there was the sound of feet outside on the gravel drive. Lian and the others were back.

The little group came round the corner of the house. They looked tired and shuffled their feet nervously. The smallest girl was asleep in Lian's arms. Tee was carrying the middle one on his back, and the eldest plodded along like a sleepwalker.

"Oh Madame, so much talking, so many new rules," Lian began, with a rush of words. "We now have a boss two houses away, and he'll tell us what to do and give us permission to do things. Each five houses make up a cell. We must grow vegetables—no more flowers—and all the trees which don't bear fruit must be chopped down. We must all raise animals for food, but we have to ask permission to kill them and then we have to share with the village. We have so much to learn! They said we must now suffer as our brothers in the North suffered all these years, while we lived like kings with the Americans. We'll have a class every night, and we'll be tested and we must not fail—how will we ever manage?"

Harry felt a strong surge of sympathy for them, and his mother and Anna each took one of the older children to get them into bed. Tee stood unmoving, his back bent as though he still carried the child. Harry patted his arm and said, "I'll make you all some tea." Tee followed him into the kitchen and stood slumped against the counter, watching as he filled the kettle and put it on to boil. "I don't think I'll be able to manage, Harry. It's so long since I was in school, and even then I was very slow at learning."

"Tee, don't worry, I'm sure the others will help you. As soon as the tea is ready, you can take cups for you and Somphong. After a good night's sleep, you'll feel better." Stout Tee nodded his head doubtfully, his usual cheerful face etched with worry and fatigue.

Spy

The plane to Bangkok was rocked and buffeted by the storm. The rain beat heavily on the small portholes as the lightening zigzagged across the black sky.

The passengers held their breath, tensely waiting for the pilot to make his third attempt to land. A chicken squawked and fluttered in its basket, a baby wailed, and the attendants anxiously watched the passengers in their care.

The plane finally touched down on the tarmac, bouncing and sliding through the teeming rain, and slowly braked to a stop before the terminal. The passengers, happily released from tension, jumped up chattering excitedly.

The Porters only had small nightbags, so they were able to leave the aircraft quickly, ahead of the families who had to gather children, parcels and livestock.

Truong, the driver from the Canadian embassy, was waiting for them. He was obviously relieved at their safe landing and whisked them away.

John, a small wiry man with a lean, craggy face and bright blue eyes, bounded down the steps of the embassy building to meet them. He puffed contentedly on an old much-loved briar pipe and clapped Harry and his Dad on their backs, and smiled at Anna.

"Great to see you all. Anna and Harry, why don't you go and find Mai in the kitchen. I know she's been busy baking all morning in anticipation of your arrival."

He grabbed Jake Porter by the arm and steered him into his office. "Jake, I've a tough assignment for you. We're in a lot of trouble."

"You are?" Jake sat down in a comfortable armchair across the desk. "Well, we almost didn't make it in that storm, but luckily our pilot must have been an old pro."

John made no comment; he frowned down at the file in front of him and puffed hard on his pipe.

"Jake, I know you've been working hard in Laos, trying to get the impossible to work. I consider your work important. I know you get on well with the people, and that your family have been readily accepted and assimilated. Of course, things are very different now with the communists, but your work in this country is apolitical. No changes will be made to your assignment, apart from those which you think are necessary. You'll continue until the end of your contract, cooperating fully. Naturally our technical experts have nothing to do with politics, and the internal government policies of the host country, etcetera . . . but sometimes one becomes involved unintentionally."

John gave Jake a long, hard stare. He stood up abruptly and began pacing the floor, puffing hard on his pipe. Jake watched in amused silence, wondering what he was leading up to that could cause the usually placid man to become so agitated.

"As I was saying, you're not involved in politics—although naturally, you must have your own views. I'm now asking your help. This is politics with a capital P, and it's dangerous. But we have no one else to do this in Laos. It's a matter of life and death. Could cause embarrassment and, quite possibly, danger to you and your family. But Jake you have to do it. I know it's a lot to ask, but you're on the spot." He paused, and looked keenly at Jake.

"Do go on, John. I don't know what you're hinting at, but I'm dying of curiosity."

"It's a long story." John sat down again at his desk. "Twelve years ago, a Canadian priest called Père Gregoire worked in Vientiane. He was an elderly Quebecois and was much thought of in Laos. He'd been there many, many years. He spoke the language like a native, considered Laos his home and the Lao his people. In all the years he was there, he never returned home. As a young man, he trained as a doctor but was called to the priesthood before qualifying. He worked among the poor families, toiling in the fields with them and treating their minor ailments. He also took in half a dozen or so homeless local youths to live with him at any one time. Among these boys was a very bright métis who dreamt of becoming a doctor. Père Gregoire encouraged him and the boy assisted in his clinic.

"Even in those days, the Russians and Chinese were vying for Indochina. Then, as now, they didn't pour in money or aid as we Westerners do. But they earnestly sought out superior students to send to Moscow or Peking to be educated and indoctrinated for the future.

"This boy, Louis Sombat, was noticed by the Chinese.

Père Gregoire was horrified and tried to dissuade him. The good father called on his superiors in Quebec for help and they, of course, were equally shocked. Very soon a place and funds were arranged for Louis in Quebec, and a passport obtained for him. Then an application was made for a Canadian visa.

"Unhappily, Père Gregoire, a garrulous old man in his eighties, was terribly excited by his protegé being whisked away from ungodly danger to the safety of Quebec, and unwittingly mentioned the young man's lucky escape to the consul. Within the week, the old priest and his protegé were summoned to the embassy where an anonymous man from Ottawa informed them that Louis Sombat should go to Peking. Later he'd be able to go to Quebec. Surely he would do this to assist Père Gregoire's country. After all the priest had been like a father to him for many years.

"The old man was in despair and the younger one was afraid, but Ottawa was not going to give up this heaven-sent opportunity to have an agent in China.

"Last year Louis, now a fully qualified and experienced doctor after twelve years behind the Bamboo Curtain, returned to Vientiane. He's still a Christian, still in the pay of Ottawa, but is also indebted to the Chinese. After a few months back he met, fell in love with, and married a charming young widow of good family—also half French. He's now the proud stepfather of two young boys.

"All was well until the takeover, but now Louis's uncle by marriage has appeared as the number-two man in the new pro-Russian government in Laos, and Louis is afraid for his family."

John paused in his narrative to empty and refill his pipe.

"What happened to Père Gregoire?" asked Jake.

"He died some years ago. He was over ninety and worked until the end. I don't think he ever forgave Ottawa."

"Poor old man," said Jake, shaking his head with regret and then, looking at John with a twinkle in his eye, asked, "and how do my family and I come into this spy story?"

John puffed heartily at his pipe to light it and then, leaning back in his chair, continued.

"Well Jake, first I want you to collect some documents tonight. Quite simple, just a matter of taking your kids out to dinner and you'll be contacted. Your family are a splendid cover and you're unknown here in Bangkok. You'll then take them to Ottawa where you will be briefed more fully. In the meantime, Anna and Harry will return home as planned—" John broke off abruptly as Harry poked his head around the door. "Hi, Harry, getting bored?"

"John, it's stopped raining, can we go swimming?"

"Sure, we've finished our business, and that sounds like a good idea."

5

Cloak-and-Dagger Stuff

By eight, they were seated at a small table in a French restaurant. It was dimly lit by small red lanterns on the tables, and the whitewashed walls were covered with faded photos of racehorses and jockeys. The small flamboyantly dressed Frenchman, lounging behind the bar, ignored them. Only one other table was occupied, by two Frenchmen who were arguing and hissing at each other in low voices between mouthfuls.

A young waitress, dressed in a silk skirt and bolero, pointed out the short menu of the day, chalked up on a blackboard. Jake ordered frogs' legs, and Anna and Harry, hors d'oeuvres, to be followed by pepper steaks, French fries and salads for them all.

Harry eagerly watched the door. First, a middle-aged couple came in, followed by a party of government officials. He wondered who would be the one to give something to his father.

The steaks were excellent, followed by cremes caramel and, for Jake and Anna, coffee. The waitress brought the bill, Jake paid and they stood up to leave. Harry was tremendously disappointed. Nothing had happened. But as they reached the door, the waitress hurried over to catch up with them, her pale face delicately flushed.

"Monsieur, your attache case!" she said, handing it to Jake.

"But Dad," cried Anna, as her father, the case in his hand, firmly pushed her through the door, "you didn't bring—"

"There's a taxi, hop in now." Jake unceremoniously pushed his children into the cab, and it moved off so quickly he barely had time to arrange his long legs and close the door.

Harry sat back with a happy smile on his face. Anna was annoyed, because she knew perfectly well the case did not belong to her father.

John met them at the side door of the Embassy, and they went up to his office, where Jake handed over the case.

"I don't understand," began Anna.

Harry laughed. "It's all cloak-and-dagger stuff, Anna. We especially went to that restaurant so Dad could be handed some papers."

"How do you know?" asked Jake.

"I heard John explaining, when I came up to get you this morning," replied Harry. "The door was open."

"Humph," snorted Jake, "some security here. Not another word, young Harry." Harry looked hurt. John was glancing quickly through several pages of handwritten notes.

"Just what we wanted," he exclaimed. "I'll make some copies for myself and you can take the originals to Ottawa."

"Ottawa?" cried Anna.

"Just me," said her father, as John hurried out from the

room. "You two will return on the plane as planned. I'll only be away a short while."

John returned with a handful of photocopies and placed them in the safe for the night. "Since your planes are early, I'll meet you at the airport. I'll have a package for you kids to take back to Vientiane, as well. A Mr Lee will collect it in the afternoon.

I have a photo of him somewhere here." John rifled through a pile of papers in the safe, selected an envelope, and pulled out a small passport-sized photo. "Have a very careful look, you must be sure to give the package only to him."

Mr Lee was elderly, with grey hair, two gold teeth and a rather large nose for an Asian.

"He's thin and tall. In fact, as tall as your father, and he's half French. Do you think you'll recognize him?"

"Yes," replied Anna and Harry in unison.

"He'll come to your house to look at the air conditioner. Once he's upstairs, you can give him the package. Be sure that no one, apart from your mother, sees the exchange. As soon as you reach home you must tell her he's coming, understand?"

"Yes."

"Is that all?" asked Harry, somewhat disappointed.

John laughed, "Yes, that's all."

6

The Package

Their mother was at the airport to meet them. "Where's your father?" she asked, looking around in surprise.

"He had to make a quick trip to Ottawa."

The customs men just nodded amiably as they passed through and, in a few minutes, they were in the car on their way home.

"Well, how was it?"

"Pretty dull," said Harry, "except for a bit of cloak-and-dagger stuff. We went to this restaurant for dinner, John had told Dad to expect some papers. All through the meal, I was waiting for someone to sidle up—but no one did!"

"I knew nothing about it, Mum, and when the waitress called after Dad to say he'd forgotten his attache case, I really put my foot in it—big time. Dad fairly shoved us out and into a taxi," continued Anna. "I hope we weren't followed—I forgot to look." Harry butted in quickly to continue the story. "Anyway, this morning John gave Dad some papers to take to Ottawa, and we have a package, which is to be collected this afternoon."

"Oh no, by whom? What are we being involved in?"

"Don't worry, Mum. A Mr Lee will come to look at the air conditioner upstairs and we'll slip him the package, when we're out of sight from spying eyes."

"We don't even have a password, but we saw his photo so we should recognize him, shouldn't we Anna?"

"Yes. I do wonder what's in the package," mused Anna, taking it out of her purse and turning it over and over. But the envelope was sealed and taped. "It's sort of cool, isn't it? But it means we'll have to stay at home all afternoon, rather than going to swim."

"He may come early and then we can still go."

"Did your father say how long he'd be away?" asked Meg.

"He thought a week or ten days, as he has to be briefed."

"Briefed?" queried Meg, surprised.

"They may send him to spy all over the place, as we're terrific cover. Most spies don't have families. They're the type who have unmemorable faces and melt into a crowd."

Meg and Harry laughed. Anna was quite right, Jake was far too large and full of life to be easily overlooked.

"Here we are," sighed Meg, as they reached home. Lian and her little girls came running to greet them. Beauty barked excitedly, making the rabbits skitter in their hutches.

"Where is Monsieur?" asked Lian, peering into the empty car.

"He's gone to Ottawa for a few days. But come and see what we've brought you from Bangkok," replied Anna, and they all eagerly followed her into the house.

After lunch, they sat on the verandah, where they had a good view of the gate, and waited for Mr Lee. Tee and Somphong were taking their siesta, while Lian was ironing in the kitchen with her little girls playing at her feet.

The afternoon passed slowly and Mr Lee did not appear. At four, their mother went in to make tea and feed the dog. Harry yawned loudly and stretched, "What a boring afternoon. I must feed the rabbits, Anna, so you stay here just in case." Anna nodded vaguely, completely immersed in her book.

Meg brought out the tea and, as she poured, she asked casually, "What happens if Mr Lee doesn't come?"

"I don't know. John didn't even think of it. I suppose we'll just have to wait until Dad returns."

"I wonder what could have happened," said Harry. "I hope he's not been arrested."

"Perhaps he never received the message about the package."

"I suppose that's possible. Perhaps he'll come tomorrow. But I hope we don't have to sit around all week waiting—that would mean no swimming."

"Harry, how could you? This must be much, much more important than our going for a swim."

Dusk fell. "He's not coming now," sighed Anna, "it would be pointless to break the curfew."

7

Sabotage

It was ten o'clock the next morning when the bell rang. Anna and Harry leapt up from the table, where they were finishing a late breakfast.

"Sit down," cautioned their mother. "Let Tee open the gate as usual."

They sat down reluctantly. After a few minutes, Tee came in alone, and handed Meg a note. Meg quickly opened it.

"What does it say, Mum?"

"Just a minute. How strange. Who brought this, Tee?"

"It was a young boy," replied Tee. "He handed it to me and ran away, without a word."

"What does it say?" demanded Harry, impatiently.

"It invites us to go to the Pagoda at eleven. There's not even a signature." Meg turned the paper over and around, hoping to find some clue to the identity of the writer, but it revealed nothing.

"Which Pagoda?"

"I should imagine it means the café."

"Well, we'd better get moving," said Harry, getting up.

"I wonder if we should go? It's decidedly odd. If it's from

your Mr Lee, why doesn't he come here—a café is so public."

"Perhaps it's a trap."

"That's what I wondered, but . . . I hope you'll recognize him."

"Sure, we've seen his photo."

"Let's go, then. But you must be one hundred percent sure before you hand over the package. You don't want to make a mistake. The note must be for us as it's written in English, and who but Mr Lee would send us a note this way?"

At eleven o'clock they were parked across the wide road from La Pagoda, an elegant tearoom that had hundreds of birdcages hanging among the bushes outside the windows.

Eleven was a busy time, when the local businessmen took a break. But the Porters found a table, and Anna and Harry ordered icecreams and their mother a coffee, after which they sat back and casually glanced about the room. There were several groups of elderly men talking quietly at nearby tables, but Mr Lee was clearly not among them. They ate their ices slowly, and still no Mr Lee appeared. By twelve, they felt they couldn't linger any longer and drove home. They were puzzled and a little apprehensive.

"I hope no one came to the house while we were out."

An excited Tee greeted them at the gate. He told them that a gentleman had come a short while ago, and he was already upstairs mending the air conditioner.

Anna and Harry leapt out of the car and charged up the stairs, expecting to see Mr Lee at last. Their mother followed more slowly, feeling uneasy. At the top of the stairs, her fears were confirmed when two frantic children whispered to her

that the man was not Mr Lee. Were they sure? Of course.
This man was much younger and had a decidedly small
nose.

Meg took a deep breath to calm her pounding heart and
walked into the room. The man, who'd been fiddling with a
screwdriver at the air conditioner case, turned and bowed.
He was in his fifties, as far as she could judge. He was neatly
dressed in a white shirt, dark trousers and sandals. His face
was thin, with hard brown eyes, a small nose and a narrow
mouth. A perfectly ordinary man, with no visible sign of
mixed blood in him.

He greeted her in French and gravely assured her that the
air conditioner was in good working order. Meg quietly
thanked him and asked how much she owed. The man
smiled slightly and shook his head. Then he turned to Anna
and Harry, who stood in defiant silence by the door.

"I believe you have a package for me?" He spoke with
authority, in accentless English.

"But you're not Mr Lee," blurted out Harry.

Meg frowned at Harry and he was silent. They stood looking at the visitor suspiciously, and he returned their stares.
Finally, the man spoke.

"I am Mr Lee. Presumably you were shown a photo—it
was of my elder brother. However, he is no longer in Vientiane. He is in Nongkhai. You may give me the package and
I will see he receives it immediately."

Nongkhai was the town across the Mekong River in
neighbouring Thailand.

"We were told to give it to your brother and no one else.
We will have to go to Nongkhai ourselves."

"Very well, as you wish." The man gave a very French shrug, but his face remained expressionless. "You will find him in the market, selling coffee."

"Thank you," said Meg.

"Bonjour, Madame," said the man and slipped noiselessly down the stairs.

"Well," said Meg, sitting down abruptly. "This is a nuisance. I suppose we'll have to go to Nongkhai tomorrow, as long as the border is open."

"Why can't we go now?" asked Harry, impatient for adventure.

"No, it's too late. We don't know how easy it will be to find him, and we have to be back before the curfew. Your Mr Lee will just have to wait one more day. His brother must have intercepted the message and come instead."

"Oh look, he left a screw out, Mum," said Anna, picking one up from the floor.

"Harry, see if you can put it back," called Meg on her way downstairs. "I don't want it really breaking down."

Harry looked carefully over the air conditioner, but could see no missing screws on the outside.

"Must be from inside," he muttered. He carefully unscrewed the front of the machine and looked inside. He gave a low whistle of surprise, "Anna, call Mum quick!"

"What is it?"

"Ssh," cautioned Harry, as he met them at the top of the stairs. He put his finger to his lips and then whispered, "We've been bugged."

They trooped into the family room, and Harry pointed dramatically inside the air conditioner. Sure enough, hidden in a corner was a listening device. Meg switched on the machine, but nothing happened. It really didn't work now.

They went downstairs and out to the verandah, without uttering a word. Their mother was extremely worried, but Anna and Harry were both bubbling with excitement. They began speculating whether perhaps the whole house was wired.

Meg realized that this could be true. Should they remove the device or not? They all agreed that it would have to be destroyed. It was unthinkable for them to live with it until Jake returned. Also, they'd have to search the whole house for others, and then call in the electrician to mend the air conditioner.

They felt very vulnerable and alone. Meg impressed upon the children not to confide in anyone, either their friends or the domestic staff. As to the mystery of the identity of the two Mr Lees, perhaps they'd find out tomorrow. That is, if they found the right Mr Lee in Nongkhai. Looking for him could turn out to be another wild-goose chase. They'd just have to wait and see.

Mr Phong the electrician sent his younger son home with them straight away. Phan Phong inspected the air conditioner and shook his head in horror, saying, "Look, the wires have been cut." His eyes darkened with concern. "Quickly, turn off the power."

Harry ran downstairs to turn off the electricity at the main switch.

"You could have been electrocuted—the wires have been deliberately cut."

It was far more serious than they'd realized.

"Who has been touching this, Madame?"

"A man came to look at it this morning," murmured Meg, feeling embarrassed, since the Phongs were their regular electricians.

"It was vandalized—you must never let anyone touch it but our family. You could have been killed. Who was this man?"

"I don't know," said Meg. "It was arranged by a friend, but once my husband returns we should be able to find out."

"You must, a man like this is a great danger. I hope he touched nothing else."

"I don't think so, but he was alone up here." Meg felt mortified.

"I'll check the whole house, just as a precaution." He repaired the air conditioner, and then, as promised, checked the rest of the house. It appeared nothing else had been touched. As Phan Phong left, he warned, "You have to be very careful now whom you let into the house. These are dangerous times. Never, never leave anyone alone, not even for one minute. You must trust no one."

They watched him cycle away. They were all upset. Perhaps this cloak-and-dagger stuff was not much fun after all.

"Who do you think that man was, Mum?"

"I really don't know, but presumably not a friend. I must think about this before we go dashing off to Nongkhai. Remember, we have to pass through customs each end, we could be searched, and if they've been tipped off the package will be found. Perhaps Mr Lee is not in Nongkhai at all.

"I wonder what's in that package, let me see it, Anna."

Anna opened her purse and handed her mother the package. It was a small yellow envelope, hard and fat.

"It must be passports. But why is John sending passports with you? . . . Of course, a great many people would like them, to be able to leave the country legally. What should we do?"

8

Nongkhai

Meg slept badly. She'd spent hours wandering around the dark, silent house, gazing out of the windows into the moonlit garden and beyond the walls towards the village, the rice paddies and the wat. Every hour the wat drum boomed hollowly, otherwise nothing moved—even the dogs were silent.

At breakfast, she told Anna and Harry what she'd decided in the early hours.

"What do you think if you both go to find Mr Lee, as you've seen his photo? You can take a taxi from the end of the road and cross to Nongkhai on the ferry. I'll stay home with the package. We might very well have another visitor, as the bug's no longer working. It will be obvious that you're not carrying the package, so no one should bother you. If you're able to speak to Mr Lee alone, you should. Otherwise don't approach him. You can try again tomorrow or we'll just have to wait until Jake gets home. What do you think?"

"Sounds great, Mum. A real adventure."

"Steady on now. It's an adventure but you must keep your wits about you. This is very important."

By nine o'clock Anna and Harry were in the taxi on the

way to the border and the ferry across to Thailand. All they
carried were their own travelling documents, some money
and a string bag. Their mother had asked them to bring back
some potatoes, and anything else they might see which was
no longer available in Vientiane.

Anna was worried and kept glancing behind to make sure
they weren't being followed. There was little traffic on the
road, which ran through a few villages, passed fields, an
army camp and some abandoned factories—their owners
having fled across the border.

They had no problems either at the checkpoint on the
road, a few miles before the ferry station, or at the dock
itself. A ferry boat rocked gently at the bottom of a long
flight of uneven, steep steps. It was just about to leave, so
Anna and Harry ran down and had to jump over several
empty boats tied together at the dock to board the ferry.

The only other passengers were two monks dressed in
orange robes and carrying furled black umbrellas, two businessmen, and some young foreigners with long straggly hair
and beads around their necks.

The crossing barely took ten minutes, and at the other side
they clambered up steep steps to the customs post in Nongkhai. As they had nothing to declare, the formalities were
brief. They signed the register and handed over their passports, which would be returned on their way back. After just
a few minutes, they were walking out into the hot sunshine
of the busy little town.

The market in Nongkhai was not large. There was a covered meat and fish section, and outside it an area for fruit and
vegetables. More stalls were huddled together on the pe-

rimeter selling clothes, shoes and a variety of other merchandise, and along the streets around the market square were stores selling leather goods, furniture, hardware and dry goods. Anna and Harry wandered around until finally, in a large corner store brimming with barrels and sacks, Harry spotted Mr Lee. He was sitting at the back of the dark store at a small desk, doing accounts with a wooden abacus. Another man was measuring out rice for a customer, while a large woman sat fanning herself at the door. Anna and Harry slowly moved to the back of the store, pretending to check out the merchandise crowding the shelves. Mr Lee looked up at them as they approached.

"Mr Lee?" asked Anna, softly.

The old man nodded. "I'm Anna Porter and this is my brother, Harry. We were expecting you at our house in Vientiane."

"You were? When was this?"

"Two days ago. But your brother came yesterday instead. At least, he said he was your brother."

"Ah," said Mr Lee. "Yes, no doubt it was my brother. Did you give him the package?"

"No. We were told to give it to you."

"That's good."

"He bugged our house."

"He did what?"

"He put a listening device in our house and cut the wires of our air conditioner. Phan Phong said we could have been electrocuted."

Mr Lee was clearly upset. "Oh I'm so sorry. Things are worse than I imagined. Do you have the package?"

"No, our mother has it at home."

"I see." Mr Lee paused and became thoughtful. "I'm leaving for Bangkok on the evening train, as I'm not able to return to Laos. My brother's betrayed both his family and his country, so be very careful. He's a communist and has become a very important man in the new government.

"The package is essential to my daughter and her family so they can leave Laos. You must deliver it to her, I can trust no one else."

Anna and Harry promised to deliver it. Mr Lee explained that they were to take the package to the family house in Vientiane, where the old family nurse was acting as caretaker. She would tell them where to find his daughter. He then went into great detail about the precise location of the house. Although, Vientiane was only a small city, with few main roads, there were hundreds of unnamed winding lanes that branched off one another, leading far away from the main arteries.

If they opened the package, Mr Lee went on, they would find the passports of his daughter Mimi and her husband Dr Louis Sombat, so they could identify them from the photographs. Mimi and the boys would leave as soon as they had their passports, since it was no longer safe for them to remain. It was up to Anna and Harry to help them. Would they do that?

"Yes, of course, we will."

Mr Lee smiled slightly, at their earnest response. "Go now and thank you." He bowed solemnly over his joined hands and returned to his accounts.

"We must hurry back home," said Anna.

"But the potatoes!"

"Quick then, let's buy some and go."

Carrying the bag between them, Anna and Harry threaded their way between the people on the narrow sidewalk. Sometimes they had to step onto the road, narrowly missing bicycles and samlaws.

There was a line-up at customs, where they waited for the return of their papers. Anna glanced around to see if they were being watched. Finally their turn came and, with their papers in their hands, they flew down the steps to the dock. The dock had risen with the river, and an overladen ferry boat was just about to be pushed off. The roof was covered with baskets of fruit, bags of plastic sandals and rolls of material—trading had not ceased completely. The cabin was full of chattering women, but Anna and Harry pushed their way through and found enough space to squat between all the packages and people's legs.

The boat moved out very slowly, the water almost slopping over the side. Anna hoped and prayed that they wouldn't sink.

They were among the first off, and they carefully carried the potatoes over the two rocking boats tied to the dock— one already filled with passengers for the return journey. When they reached the top of the steps, they were greeted by the tantalizing smell of food. It was only then that they realized what a long time it had been since they'd eaten breakfast and how extremely hungry they were. They turned along a narrow path which led to several outdoor restaurants, which were balanced precariously on stilts over the water. They stopped at one of these and were in the process of choosing two pieces of delicious-looking chicken roasting on a spit, when a shot rang out. It was followed by the sound of running feet and shouting coming their way. Another shot went whistling past close to them, and Anna, Harry and the proprietor dived down behind a table. A young man, gasping for breath, rushed past them and vaulted over the half wall to the river below. A few seconds later there was a splash as he hit the water. Boots clumped past the crouching kids, as four Pathet Lao soldiers went running in pursuit. The soldiers were shouting with excitement and firing haphazardly. Above the noise came the sound of a motor as the escaped man was taken across the river. The soldiers, furious at loosing their quarry, fired at the fleeing boat. But the boat seemed to continue on course and out of range. The soldiers kept up a fusillade of bullets until their supply was exhausted and, only then, did they turn and tramp back to the customs building, chattering excitedly.

The elderly restaurant proprietor calmly patted her hair back into place and carefully wrapped in a large leaf the two pieces of chicken which Anna and Harry had selected for themselves. They eagerly ate the chicken as they went in search of a taxi, the juice running unchecked in greasy rivulets down their chins.

9

The Lee House

Meg was about to sit down to a solitary lunch when Anna and Harry arrived.

"That was well timed," cried Meg, as the children sat down to a second lunch. "Any luck, did you find him?"

"Yes."

"Well?"

Anna and Harry took turns in recounting the events of the morning, concluding, "Mr Lee's brother, the one who came here, is a communist and doesn't want his niece and family to leave. He must have intercepted the message and hoped to get the passports. And now it's up to us to deliver them so Mr Lee's daughter and her children can leave."

"We must be careful. But first, let's have a look at them."

There were four passports. One old and three new. The older one showed a serious young man, Louis Sombat, whose age was given as thirty-five, and profession as an accountant, and whose passport had been issued in Paris two years previously. The others' passports were only months old and issued in Bangkok. The young woman was very pretty with delicate features and a long straight nose. The two small boys stared solemnly straight ahead at the camera.

"How strange," murmured Meg, turning them over.

"Do you suppose they're fake?" asked Anna.

"You bet," cried Harry, excitedly, "because I know for sure that this Louis is a doctor not an accountant."

"Well, that doesn't concern us, Harry," Meg gently told her son. "Our job is to deliver them. Do you think you'll recognize them from these passport photos?"

They studied the photos carefully, noting the eyes, noses and mouths in particular, until they were sure they would recognize the people. Meg then told them the plan for the afternoon.

"We'll go swimming, but on the way we'll visit the Medlicotts to say goodbye. They're due to leave in a day or two and, just by chance, they live up the same lane as the Lees. So we have a great excuse to calmly drive up there, visit the Medlicotts and then walk down to speak to the caretaker. Can you be ready in half an hour?" Anna nodded in agreement, and Harry got up quickly and said, "I must go and tell Tee about the shooting."

"What shooting? You never mentioned shooting!"

Harry grinned mischievously, and with a cocky wave left Anna to tell the story.

The Medlicotts were delighted to have visitors. They had been sorting and packing all day, and welcomed an excuse to sit down and relax for half an hour.

"We have to leave behind so much," wailed Betty Medlicott, "although the children wish to part with nothing. But at least Anan and Lee will be able to open a stall at the market with all the odds and ends. I'm so sorry to be leaving this house. I've never lived in such a pretty place, but all our neighbours have left and we'll be the last to go.''

"Do you know who owns the house with the huge trees and grey gate?'' asked Meg casually.

"It's a local family, I only know them to pass the time of day with. I haven't seen them for the last few days, I think they may have left. There's a terrible old caretaker who shrieks at us when we pass the gate.''

"It must be a lovely old house, I might go and see if we can take a look, especially if you think it's empty.''

"You're not thinking of moving are you?''

"No, but I love looking at houses, and once you've left I'll probably never come up here again.''

Meg, Anna and Harry walked down the narrow, rutted lane. There were high walls on either side over which hung willows.

The grey gate was solid and there were no gaps through which they could see. Meg pushed the bell. Nothing happened. They could hear ducks behind the gate but no human sounds. Meg rang a second time. Still nothing. She banged sharply on the gate. They heard a door creak open and the slop, slop of sandals, and an angry voice muttering as the person drew closer.

"Here she comes,'' whispered Anna, backing away from the gate.

"Who's there?'' a cracked voice called.

"Friends from Mr Lee in Nongkhai,'' replied Meg softly. "We want to speak to Dr Louis.''

The gate opened slowly, and an old woman peered out suspiciously.

"Come in quickly," she croaked, pulling the gate open a little wider for them to slip through. She glanced up and down the deserted lane before putting her shoulder to the heavy gate. Harry helped her push it shut, and they followed her into the house.

The room they entered was large and dark. The wooden shutters were closed and it was sparsely furnished. Two beautiful Siamese cats stalked proudly from the shadows and entwined themselves around Meg's legs. The old woman peered at the Porters in the dim light.

"Eh bien, you come from François?" she muttered. "Je ne sais pas. I don't know rien. Louis and Mimi are not able to live here any more, mais c'est possible que Louis viendra ce soir. He brings food for the cats and me."

"But the curfew?" interrupted Anna. The old woman glared and spat expertly into a spittoon in the corner.

"You tell me where you live and I will see Louis comes to you before dawn. These days he is very busy, there are so many sick, especially the old and the babies. You have the passports for them, huh?"

"Yes," said Harry.

"Good, c'est bien—they must go. Every day it becomes more dangerous. I will miss them though. I will never see them again. I was the boys' nurse—they are like my own. A pity Michel turned out so bad, but it happens in the best of families."

"But they are just little . . . " protested Meg.

"Ah, I don't mean Mimi's sons," the old nurse croaked. "Mais non, mes garçons sont François et Michel. François is a good man, like his father before him. A family man, a

grandfather. But Michel's head has always been full of politics. He is a communist," and she spat again, the jet of red
liquid landing squarely in the spittoon. "Tell me, how is
Louis to reach your house?"

Meg gave her the directions. The old woman nodded—
she knew the area. "As soon as he comes, I will send him to
you. He is a good boy, a worthy husband for little Mimi.
François is a clever man, I knew he would get them away."

"What about you?" asked Meg.

"Eh bien, I'm too old to travel. I used to go to France with
the family, but now I will stay here until I die. I look after
the house and the cats. Michel comes to bother me now and
again and, of course, once Mimi has gone this house will be
his. He is the younger son and was brought up a Catholic.
Maintenant il est un saleau rouge, and will surely go au
diable comme sa grandmaman always threatened."

"Isn't Monsieur François a Catholic, too?" asked Anna,
in surprise.

"Mais non," shrieked the old woman, "he is a Buddhist.
The elder son is always a Buddhist."

A car horn sounded loudly in the lane.

"Sacre bleu," cried the old woman in alarm. "Here is
trouble." There was a banging at the gate, and someone with
a loud voice demanded to be let in. The old nurse's hand
trembled on Meg's arm, and the two cats streaked into the
shadows to hide under a heavy brocade couch.

"It is Michel, he must not see you here. He won't stay
long. Quick, you must hide," gasped the old woman, pluck-
ing at Meg's sleeve in agitation. She shuffled into the back
of the house, and they followed her into a small cell-like

room with a single bed.

"Stay here while I get rid of him."

There was more banging and shouting at the gate. The Porters heard the sound of the old woman's sandals, and her angry muttering turned to a high-pitched scream, "Why are you so impatient? Now that you are a dirty communist, have you lost your manners? I'm an old woman, I sleep in the heat of the day. Have some patience, Michel. In love of your father's name have some patience."

The old nurse slowly opened the gate, but the man pushed it impatiently sending her staggering.

"Stand back, old woman. I'm bringing my car in, so let me open both gates."

"Why must you bring your car in here?" she shrieked. "Can you not leave me in peace?"

"I am coming to live here now."

"You are what? This is not your house!" she cried.

"Yes, it is. My dear brother has left the country and his daughter is no longer in residence here. I'm a man of importance now and this is my house."

The old woman turned and shuffled back into the house muttering darkly. The Porters heard her going into the kitchen next door, and then they heard the creak of a chair. Quick footsteps came into the house.

"Old woman, old woman," Michel called harshly.

"Yes," sighed the old nurse, as the man stopped in the doorway.

"I don't need you here. You are too old to work, and I have two young soldiers coming to look after me. You must go."

"Go?" whispered the old woman.

"Yes, pack up your things and go!"

"But where am I to go? I have always lived here. I came here before you were born. I have nowhere to go."

"Go, go. I don't care where you go. Take those cats too, I can't stand them. I'm going upstairs to sleep. I want to find the house empty when I wake. Do you understand?"

The Porters looked at each other in horror. The poor old nurse. There was no sound from the kitchen. They heard the man's footsteps as he climbed up the uncarpeted stairs and then there was silence.

The Porters waited, but the old woman didn't come. Meg quietly opened the door, signalling the children not to move. She tiptoed out into the kitchen. The woman was hunched in a corner on a backless old chair. She didn't hear or see Meg, as tears silently fell down the furrows of her wrinkled cheeks. Meg went over to her and gently touched her arm. The nurse looked up in surprise. She had forgotten them.

"Did you hear that communist?" she growled. "Throwing me out of this house after more than sixty years." She angrily rubbed away her tears.

"Gently, gently," said Meg, "you'll come home with us. Collect your belongings and the cats. I will go and fetch the car."

The children, the old nurse and the cats were waiting at the gate as Meg drove up. They quickly put the bundles into the car. The cats scrabbled and yowled indignantly under a blanket in a wicker shopping basket. Meg helped the old woman into the front seat, with the cat's basket on her knee. "Quick children, in you get," Meg urged, glancing up nerv-

ously at the shuttered windows of the old house. She wondered whether their departure was being observed. Of
course, if Monsieur Michel was watching he would know
exactly where the old woman was being taken.

At the end of the lane, the old woman suddenly cried out.
Meg stopped the car abruptly. "What is it?"

"I'll not be able to give Louis the message. What are we
to do?"

10

Stakeout

"What are we going to do?" asked Anna. Louis would have
to be stopped before he reached the house, and there was
also the problem of the curfew. Meg didn't want to involve
the Medlicotts, who were British diplomats and on the verge
of leaving, but their property was perfectly situated between
the paddyfield, from which Louis would approach, and the
Lee house. From the comparative safety of the Medlicott's
garden, they might be able to intercept Louis before he
walked into a trap.

After much discussion, it was decided that Anna and
Harry would hide in the garden for the night, while Meg
would stay at home with the passports. They would tell Lian
that they were spending the night with friends because of the
curfew.

Meg then turned to Nurse. But she had sat in a daze while
they talked, neither listening nor drinking from the glass on
the table in front of her.

"Nurse," said Meg quietly, "do you understand our
plan?"

Nurse moved her head in bewilderment and croaked,

"You must talk to Louis."

"We will," promised Harry.

While Lian was settling Nurse in her new room, Harry and Anna went to collect warm clothing, as it might be cool sitting in a garden all night.

Meg went into the kitchen to prepare a picnic supper for them. She had a can of tuna hidden away for a special occasion. This evening was special, although hardly the kind of special evening she had envisaged for opening the can. There were also a few remaining bottles of Coke left, bought before the factory had failed to open one morning at the start of the week.

"Are you ready?"

"Yes, coming," said Harry, staggering in under a pile of sweaters and sleeping bags. Anna followed with a large flashlight and a wooden Lao truncheon.

"What's that for?" asked Meg, raising her eyebrows.

"We have to have a weapon. I don't know who might jump out at us from the bushes in the dark, and I can bonk them on the head."

Meg looked worried. It could be dangerous. But after all they were only going to be at the bottom of a friend's garden, and a message had to be given to Louis before he unknowingly walked into a trap.

"Come on, Mum," said Anna soothingly, "stop worrying. We'll be alright. I just hope he does come tonight, 'cause we don't seem to be making much headway."

Betty Medlicott opened the door and gasped in surprise, "Meg, how lovely, but I'm afraid we're just about to leave, a farewell drink at HE's—no time for dinner with this wretched curfew."

"I'm not stopping, Betty. I just need one minute of your time, George's too, if he is there?"

"Yes, of course. Come in. George, George! . . ."

George, tall and balding, came hurrying down the long passage in his shirt sleeves.

"Hello, Meg. What can I do for you?"

"I know you're in a hurry, so I won't go into a long explanation but . . ."

"Yes," said Betty, laughing, "but?"

"Well, if you agree, Anna and Harry will spend the night camping by your gate. They have to intercept a man before he reaches the Lee house down the lane. I'll be back to fetch them at seven in the morning."

"My goodness," said Betty, "what are you up to?"

"Jake still away, I suppose," said George gloomily.

"Yes, he is. This is sort of official, although not involving you Brits but Canadians, I know. We don't want to involve you, but your garden is a terrific stakeout and we do have to stop this man from walking into a trap."

"You were lying to me this afternoon, Meg Porter," said Betty.

"Yes, Betty, I was," admitted Meg. "I just didn't want to involve you when you're about to leave. Anna and Harry have food, sleeping bags and strict instructions not to leave the garden, as we don't want them running into a patrol."

"Good God, no," said George with feeling. "Fine Meg, we'll keep an eye on them as soon as we're back. Are you ready, Betty? We must go, otherwise there'll not be time for even one drink!"

An hour and a half later, dusk had deepened into night and the Medlicotts returned. George Medlicott told them there was a patrol stationed at the end of the lane, and all seemed quiet at the Lees' house.

"Be very quiet, you don't want the patrol to hear you— although I doubt whether they'll come up this far. Any problems come and bang on my window." He indicated a large window at the end of the low, white house. "And don't leave the garden, is that clear?" Anna nodded in agreement.

"Yes, Sir," said Harry, wondering whether he should salute.

The moon was shining brightly and so, apart from shadows made by trees and walls, they could clearly see up and down the lane. It was very quiet as there was no traffic, and the only sound was distant radio music and a baby crying.

"I'm hungry." Anna said.

They ate their sandwiches with some cold rice and salad, and washed it all down with Coke. They decided to keep the fruit until later.

The lights went off in the house behind them, and a gate creaked open further down the lane, but no one appeared. After a while, they heard several people coming up the lane. Someone hawked loudly, and there was a rattle of metal. They saw four young soldiers approaching. But they only went as far as the Lees' house, where they crouched down on their heels to chat with someone in the gateway. The gate was being kept open. After half an hour they stood up, stretched, and walked back down the road.

A drum sounded in a wat near by, and there was the sound of a truck on the main road. It stopped at the end of the lane, then continued on again after a few minutes.

"Checking on the patrol, I expect," whispered Harry. Anna nodded, never taking her eyes off the grass and rice standing tall at the top of the lane.

"They don't seem to be worried that he'll come from this direction," she whispered. "I hope there's not a patrol on the far side of the paddy field."

"Even if there is, he should be able to slip through in the dark."

Another hour passed. They munched some fruit, and the patrol came down again and went as far as the grey gate. They did not loiter this time, just had a quick word before retracing their steps. The truck passed by again. No one came from across the paddy field.

"I'm getting stiff and bored," complained Harry.

"Go and walk around the garden on the grass," suggested Anna, "and when you come back, I'll go. My legs feel stiff too, and if we suddenly have to jump up, I don't think I'd be able to move."

Harry walked away into the garden. The lights were off in the house, although it was brightly illuminated by the moon. Harry looked at his watch: only twelve-thirty. He felt as if he had been there for a whole night, not just a few hours. He hoped Louis would come soon, though he thought it would probably not be until three or four, just before dawn when the world stands still.

He walked three times around the lawn and returned to Anna. Nothing. He stood in the shadow of a bush, and Anna crept away up the grass verge of the driveway. Harry looked up and down the lane—nothing, not even a dog. They seemed to be respecting the curfew as well—"Probably afraid their punishment would be a stew pot," he giggled to himself.

Anna returned silently, and they had the last bottle of Coke between them. Anna suddenly put a finger to her lips, her head cocked to one side as she listened intently. She sniffed the air. Someone was smoking nearby. Something moved in the shadows, between the grey gate and their hiding place. They could see the glow of a cigarette end. Suddenly the smoker seemed to have reached the end of the cigarette and threw it down on the ground. The red embers flared briefly before being stamped out and the man returned to the gateway, keeping to the shadows.

"They're as alert as we are. It'll be a close thing. If we call Louis, they'll hear and perhaps shoot. Then they'll come into the garden and find us. We mustn't make a sound. But how do we attract his attention?"

"The lane isn't very wide, and he's bound to stick to the shadows. Let's just hope he chooses this side rather than the other. We'll have to stand at the gate and grab him."

"I hope he won't be armed, he might shoot or knife us!"

"When we grab him, we must also whisper his name. It'll only be a matter of luck if the people in the gateway don't see us."

"We'd better stand at the gate then—one on either side, in the shadows."

They moved quietly into their new positions, just in time before the patrol came swiftly down the lane. This time they stopped and crouched down to have tea, prepared by someone at the gate. They seemed in no hurry. They sipped the tea, talking and laughing quietly. After what seemed a long time, they hastily leapt up, shuffling their feet and clearing their throats nervously. A stern, low voice could be heard.

"Must be Monsieur Michel ticking them off," giggled Harry.

"Sssh,"

The patrol disappeared down the lane. There was a clinking sound as the tea bowls were collected, then the gate was closed.

Suddenly Harry saw a movement from the rice paddy. He gestured excitedly to Anna. Nothing moved. They held their breaths, tense with anticipation. Then a slight sound came from a few yards away in the shadows. Before they could move, a figure materialized a few feet from them. It stopped abruptly, as though aware of their presence.

"Louis," called Anna softly. "Louis."

The figure stood motionless. They saw the gleam of a knife.

"Louis," whispered Anna desperately. A man stepped into their gateway. The knife was held poised, ready to strike.

"Yes," he hissed, moving back into the bushes. Anna and Harry followed. Anna lead them onto the grass in front of the house, so they could see the man's face in the moonlight. It was Louis. He looked very tired. His hair was longer and his face was camouflaged with black streaks. He was wearing a simple peasant suit of black trousers and shirt.

"Well?" he demanded, staring back at them.

"We've been waiting for you. You must not go to the house, Michel Lee is there, with soldiers, waiting for you."

"Oh no, what of Nurse?"

"She's alright. She's at our house, and the cats too. We brought your passports from Bangkok."

"You did. Excellent. Where are they?"

"Mum has them at the house—you must come and collect them."

"I won't be able to come to your house as it's bound to be watched, especially with Nurse there. Let me think. Where can we meet tomorrow so you can bring them to me?" He squatted down silently. "It is becoming more and more difficult to move around. They are close on my tail and I must get my family out. We cannot delay any longer. And now there's Nurse. She wouldn't think of coming with us, she said she'd stay at the house—that's why Mimi left her the cats to keep her company. Why did she leave now?"

"Michel Lee turned her out this afternoon."

"That man. He has no sense of family. He's a true communist—the State above everything. Nurse must come with us, but how to obtain her papers?" The man looked so upset that Anna said, "She'll be safe with us in Saladang."

"Yes, yes, I'm sure. But she can't stay indefinitely, although for the time being she'll have to, until we can get papers." He stood up abruptly. "I must not stay. Take this for Nurse," he pulled a package out of his shoulder bag. "Just a little meat, I could not carry more and it is slightly damp from the field. Now, tomorrow we will meet at ten in the Morning Market. I'll be dressed like this, with a large hat, and I'll be selling lettuce. You'll buy some and hand me a basket with the passports in it. I can take them out as I put the lettuce in. Clear?"

The children nodded. Louis jumped up and vanished into the shadows. There was no sound from the lane so he hadn't been noticed.

Anna and Harry fetched their sleeping bags and crept up to the verandah to sleep for a few hours. Although they thought they'd never be able to sleep for all the excitement of the day, they fell asleep almost immediately. So they did not hear the patrol as it belatedly decided to walk up to the end of the lane as far as the paddy field.

11

Handover

Meg slept fitfully. She was worried about the children and whether they would be able to intercept Louis. At dawn she fell into a deep sleep, only to be awakened by an anxious Lian half an hour later.

"Madame, come quick, the old lady is sick."

The old nurse was propped up in the corner of her bed against a pile of pillows, gasping for air. Meg took her hand, which was hot, and she noticed that her forehead was bathed in sweat. She opened her eyes briefly, but was unable to speak.

"I must fetch a doctor," said Meg. "Stay with her Lian, I'll be as quick as I can."

Within half an hour, she was parking outside the crumbling hospital buildings. Even so early in the morning, people were already sitting on benches in the long corridors. Meg was lucky, because as she turned into the doctors' passage she saw Soeur Marie, a large, kindly nun, bustling along in her starched habit.

"Bonjour, ma soeur, I have a serious problem. Is Doctor Than here?"

"Mais non, c'est trop tôt pour le jeune medecin, Madame. Quelle est votre probleme?" Meg quickly explained.

"Eh bien, c'est grave." Soeur Marie looked around, sighted an orderly at the end of the passage, and told him to run to the doctor's quarters and tell him to come immediately for an emergency. The young round-faced orderly hurried off into the overgrown garden at the end of the verandah.

"Assayez-vous donc, Madame. En dix minutes, le jeune docteur sera ici, et puis, il peut venir directement chez vous."

"Merci beaucoup, ma soeur."

The sister hurried off to organize her wards. The hospital was overcrowded and medicine was becoming scarcer by the day.

In a short while, the doctor came, still buttoning his white coat. Meg knew him well, he was a good doctor trained in Eastern Europe. She hurriedly explained about Nurse as they went out to the car.

"It sounds like heart failure, I'm afraid. Many old people are dying. They have been defeated after all these years of war. Many of them have lost the will to live, especially those who feel they are a burden to their families—they die so their families may leave."

Meg lead the doctor to the old lady's room. Lian rose from beside the bed and greeted the doctor. He gently examined Nurse, and gave her a shot from his small, black bag.

"There she'll breath more easily now. I will return this evening."

Dr Than joined Meg for breakfast, which he eat ravenously, before she drove him back to the hospital on her way to fetch Anna and Harry.

At a quarter to ten, they were in the market.

"Alright, please take a basket and buy salad and fruit while I go in search of some meat." Meg turned quickly into the dim passage between stalls of clothing, shoes and smuggled or stolen canned goods, hoping that if they were being watched, she would be followed rather than the children.

Anna and Harry wandered slowly between the fruit and vegetable stalls, stopping to look at the flowers, the coconut shredding machine, and two large baskets of fluffy baby rabbits. Anne knelt to stroke the quivering bundles of soft fur while Harry glanced at his watch. Still a few minutes to go. Of course, it might take some time to find Louis amongst the crowd of identically dressed country folk crouching beside their baskets of produce.

Most of the men were elderly and politely greeted the children as they passed. Their baskets were filled with lettuce, cucumbers, radishes, sweet potatoes and mint. Spread out on the ground in front of them, in neat rows, were frogs-on-sticks, snake steaks, some venison and bats.

"I can't see him," muttered Harry, looking around casually.

"We can go around again," suggested Anna, smiling at an old man offering her a large bunch of spring onions.

"I see him," said Harry.

"Don't hurry," cautioned Anna, as she bought the onions. Harry impatiently waited as his sister paused to buy mint from a skinny old woman with red betel juice running down her chin. Then they strolled over to Louis and peered critically at his basket of lettuce.

"They look fresh," said Harry.

"They *are* fresh," responded Louis, with a twinkle in his eyes.

"Please give me several then," said Anna, handing over her basket.

"Your nurse is dying," she whispered. "Dr Than says she'll probably not last the night."

Louis's expression did not change as he handed back the basket filled with lettuce.

"As soon as my family are on their way, I will come," he promised.

On returning home, they found that the old lady had slept peacefully all morning. Anna helped Lian put away their shopping and Meg exchanged places with Somphong, who'd sat with Nurse in case she woke, so that she could go shopping for fresh vegetables and prepare her midday rice. Meg found the tranquillity around her soothing. The cats lay stretched out asleep on the cool, concrete floor. What a deceptive peace.

It was hot after lunch, thunder boomed in the distance and the air was heavy with the smell of approaching rain. Meg, Anna and Harry waited expectantly all afternoon at home, but Louis did not come.

12

A Funeral

The deluge lasted all night. The rabbits had to be brought into the house and shut in separate bathrooms so they wouldn't fight and would be out of reach of the cats. Rain seeped through the wooden shutters and clattered on the tin roof. The old nurse lay in a deep sleep, hardly breathing, her face calm and beautiful. As the rain slowly relented, just before the break of dawn, she quietly stopped breathing.

The cats, who had sat silently in the feeble light, stood up and stretched—their vigil was over. They walked over to the door, twitching their tails, and yowled plaintively to be let out into the cool new morning. Meg watched their stately progress until they vanished into the undergrowth. She silently knelt in prayer and then crept up to her own bed for a few hours sleep.

Lian and Somphong prepared the old nurse for her last journey. The litter was covered with gold and silver paper, delicate paper flowers, a money tree and other symbols of her needs for her future life.

The village elders and the saffron-robed priests came to accompany her to the wat, where she would be cremated.

Meg and the children watched the procession meander down the little lane towards the wat, which stood calm and dignified and ancient in its circle of trees.

As Meg was preparing tea, Lian came in to tidy the kitchen. Meg told her not to bother, but Lian needed to be busy, feeling disturbed and upset after the funeral.

"You know, Madame, the man who came to repair the air conditioner was there. I'm sure it was the same man."

"Yes, it would have been the same man, Lian. She was his nurse and he threw her out of the family house after sixty years—that's why she came here."

So Michel came to the funeral, thought Meg. Did he have a guilty conscience or some sentimental feeling left in him, after all? More likely he'd hoped to find family members present. But how had he known? And what of Louis and his family? There had been no sign of them. She hoped nothing had happened to them. It was scary and she felt helpless. However, life had to go on, and now the two cats were here to stay. Food was getting more difficult to find, but they just had to live a day at a time and try not to worry about the future.

13

A Plea for Help

Anna and Harry gave their father an enthusiastic welcome when he arrived home. But they could only show minimal interest in his trip and the gifts he had brought back, unable to contain themselves for very long, and soon they were telling him all about the week's events. They concluded with their fears for the safety of Louis and his family.

Jake listened attentively and threw in a few questions here and there, and then he sat back in his chair gloomily to ponder over their bizarre story. This Michel Lee seemed to know exactly what the Porters were doing, so they must be under close watch. That probably meant that Louis was not in custody.

"But what about his wife and children, Dad?" asked Anna, when he voiced his thoughts aloud. "Do you think they've been arrested?"

"No, they would not arrest them, as they're of no special interest except as a link to Louis. With luck, they may well have managed to leave the country. However, from what you've told me, it seems Louis is on the run for some reason. Perhaps because someone suspects Louis is working for

Canada or thinks he's working for the Chinese—which, of course, he's probably obliged to do.

"Père Gregoire's orphan Louis Sombat has become deeply entangled in international intrigue. The final irony is that Michel Lee is his uncle by marriage!"

Anna and Harry listened intently as their father told them more about Louis Sombat and Michel Lee. They were not surprised, just more troubled at the fate of the little family.

Jake had been told in Ottawa that Louis Sombat had decided to continue his medical work in Laos, as long as his family were given help to leave. He was desperately needed in his country as there were very few Lao or foreign doctors left. He had decided to continue on in his clinic and send reports back to Ottawa via Jake. If things became too dangerous, he would inform Jake and he'd be spirited away to Quebec—goal of his youthful dreams.

They were all really worried, but all they could do was wait. Jake glanced around at his dispirited family, "Anyway, cheer up, I've just arrived home. I propose we go for a swim."

"Can we leave the house?"

"Of course. You can't sit at home forever waiting for Louis to appear. If he should come, Lian can tell him when we'll be back."

Anna went into the kitchen, where Lian was busy ironing. Lian's gentle face was puckered with concern as she confided that there was another re-education meeting at the wat in the evening.

"Leave the children at home with us, Lian. I'll be happy to babysit."

"Oh thank you, that would really help. Tee and Som-phong find the studying very difficult because they had so little schooling. If all our group don't pass the tests, everyone will have to start again, which would be so humiliating."

"Oh Lian, that's bad. Can you help them?"

"Yes, I will. We'll go over everything before the meet-ing."

"Leave the ironing, Mum and I can do it later. Please go and help them now."

Anna watched Lian neatly put away the ironing before hurrying out of the kitchen and calling for Tee and Som-phong. Tee came lumbering out from his doorway, with his hair rumpled and yawning hard. Anna smiled to herself. Poor Tee, he would have to miss his siesta, which would be as good a reason as any for him to hate communism.

Jake came into the kitchen, "Ready? What's the joke?"

"It's poor Tee having to return to school. He's evidently finding it very hard."

"I'm sure he is—he's a lazy devil at the best of times."

"Let's go then, we must be back before six-thirty as I'm babysitting."

*

As they approached the market in Vientiane, they became horribly aware of the sound of loud martial music.

"What can be happening?"

"Haven't you see them?"

"Seen what?" chorused the children.

"The loudspeakers," replied their father. "They have

been installed on the highest building on each block and spews out continuous propaganda and music."

"They must have gone up during the night, they certainly weren't there yesterday."

The noise was deafening.

"Look at the billboard," cried Anna, suddenly.

A huge billboard had been constructed to fill an empty corner lot at the crossroads. It showed a muscular Pathet Lao conqueror chasing and killing small, verminlike Yankee imperialists.

They had hardly time to take in all the overnight changes at the market, before their attention was drawn to a small procession led by an energetic drummer. Behind him, surrounded by a group of young men and women, came a terrified, wide-eyed man with a shaven head and a sign hanging around his neck. Following him were more young people, holding up a banner fluttering with dollar bills.

"What has he done, Dad?" whispered Anna in horror, as the procession passed.

"He worked for the Americans," said Jake softly.

"Wow, what will they do to him?" asked Harry.

"I don't know."

It was a relief to arrive at the club where everything appeared normal. However, as they climbed out of the car, a young man approached Jake.

"Sir, I was Mr Medlicott's gardener. I'm staying at the house until the owner returns, and . . ."

"Yes?" said Jake, as the man hesitated.

"Some days ago, a young woman with two small boys came asking for you. She knew you were a friend of Mr

Medlicott, and she asked me where you lived, but I didn't know. She said you knew her husband and she needed to speak to you urgently. So I said that I would try to find out from the Embassy where you lived. But the Embassy would not tell me anything—only that sometimes you came here to swim in the afternoons. So I have been coming everyday, and now at last you have come!" He broke off, with a smile of relief.

"It must be Louis's wife and children," said Meg.

Jake nodded. "Probably. How will you contact her?" he asked the gardener.

"She comes every evening just before curfew, so she cannot live far away."

"Good. I'll come to your house this evening, well before curfew. If she doesn't come by the time I have to leave, I'll give you directions to my house."

"Yes, Sir. She'll be very happy. She has been sad."

"Oh, dear," said Meg, "that doesn't sound good."

"She's alright, Madam. But I think she has a problem—although she didn't tell me—people don't trust each other, it's bad. But I understand, she has two small boys to think about." The young man sighed and with a shy smile left them.

The pool was a blaze of colour, as the Porter family strolled down the steps. All of the Western community remaining in town seemed to be there. The adults were sitting around the pool while the children were having a rowdy game in the water with a huge, multicoloured ball. Harry and Anna changed and dived in to join the fun.

*

The Medlicotts' old house stood shuttered and forlorn, and even the garden looked neglected.

Meg climbed out of the car and rang the bell. After a short pause, the gardener came jogging around the corner of the house followed by several small children. He unlocked the heavy padlock and opened the gates. Jake drove behind the house out of sight.

They were shown into the dimly lit sitting room to wait. The curious children hung around the doorway, staring at them.

"She should be here soon. I'll not open the shutters, as someone might notice—there are eyes everywhere these days." Then, giving Jake a rather furtive glance, he muttered, "I know who she is now. My wife recognized her—she used to live down the road. She is François Lee's daughter. But she doesn't live at the house any more—it is a Pathet Lao house now."

Jake nodded. The gardener, expecting an answer, was flustered and muttered angrily, "My wife thought I should tell you. I did not recognize her, because she would never walk in the lane. I would only glimpse her in the car."

"Thanks," said Jake. "I realized who she was too. I didn't say anything, thinking how in a small town everyone knows people by sight, at least."

A bell rang. "Here she is," said the gardener and made a move towards the door, scattering the two kids.

Meg quickly stood up and walked over to the shuttered

window, to peer through the slats.

"It looks like her," she said, "and the two boys."

She left the window to stand by Jake. The gardener ushered in the young mother and her children. She hesitated a moment in the doorway, alarmed to see such a large "felang" man. The little boys sensed her fear, and hung back, their eyes round with surprise. Meg stepped forward quickly to greet them, and they all bowed shyly.

"We're Meg and Jake Porter." said Jake.

"I am Louis's wife and these are my sons." The little boys were too shy to look up from studying their sandals.

"Let's sit down," said Meg. They sat in a circle on the wooden floor. The little boys sat immobile on either side of their mother—and so close, they were one unit.

"Louis brought us the passports, thank you," she bowed her head briefly. "He said we must leave immediately, and he was going to visit Nurse."

"He never came," said Meg.

"I know. We were about to leave—we had arranged a boat—but then a friend came to tell us he'd just seen Louis being arrested. I can't go without knowing what has happened to him, but I've not been able to find out anything. I'm so afraid for my boys. I know that every day it will become more difficult to escape. My boys must not stay here—but I cannot leave without news of my husband."

"But you must," said Jake. "I'll try to find your husband, but I don't know whether we will be able to secure his release," Jake spoke quietly but sharply. Madame Louis flinched.

"I cannot go," she said, with finality. "However, now my

boys have their passports. I know you have already done so much for us, but I beg you to take my boys to their uncle in France."

"You want us to take them?"

"Yes, please. Then, once I have Louis out of custody, we can follow. He couldn't remain here any longer, could he?"

"No, but he may be sent to a re-education camp—it may be months, or even years, before he is released."

"I know. But what can I do?" she said, wringing her hands. The little boys sat without expression and didn't move.

"Do the boys know their uncle?" asked Meg.

"Yes, he's my brother. He has only been there a few months."

"Do you know whether he has a job?"

In much distress, she explained that they had heard nothing from him since he had left Vientiane. Jake tried to reason with her, telling her that it would be very expensive living in France, especially Paris. And what if her brother had been unable to find work? Mimi would not listen. Her mind was made up. Of course, her brother would look after his nephews. He would find money. Also, she was sending some US dollars with the boys. She opened the passports to show Meg and Jake a small amount of precious dollar bills. Anyway, the boys were only two small extra mouths to feed, if she went too, that would be one more. Jake and Meg looked at each other. They were not going to be able to dissuade her, her mind was made up.

"We could go to Pattaya," said Meg. Pattaya was a seaside town outside Bangkok, in Thailand.

"Tomorrow?" asked Jake.

"Yes," said Meg, her mind racing, already compiling a list of things to do before they could leave. "I don't see why not."

"It would be far better if you went as well," said Jake to Madame Louis, "and I will search for Louis discreetly."

"No," she said firmly. "I am staying here."

Meg sighed and looked at her husband, who shrugged resignedly.

"Very well, as you wish, but I think it is foolish."

Mimi looked directly at him and blushed before looking down at her pale clenched fists in her lap. "I wish."

They all stood up and Madame Louis gently pushed the two little boys over to Meg.

"Take them and go now, please."

Meg took two unresisting hands and walked out of the room. Jake followed, after one final backward glance at the pale, anxious face of Madame Louis Sombat.

14

Inscrutable

Anna sat reading in a pool of light, outside Lian's little girls' room. All three were sleeping soundly together in one bed. Their usual pale cheeks were slightly flushed.

Anna had enjoyed getting them ready for bed. She had read them a story, in English, with the help of lots of bright illustrations, and they'd poured over these—lots of little fingers stroking the pages and pointing, accompanied by lots of giggles. She'd then sung "Incey Wincey Spider" and "This Little Pig Went to Market" with lots of tickling, giggles and demands for more. It had taken her some time to finally settle them down to sleep. But once they were quiet, they found it hard to keep their bright little eyes open for long.

Harry had no interest in small girls and had spent the time doing fast turns on his bicycle on the gravelled drive. He was so absorbed that he did not hear the approaching car until the lights flooded the garden.

"They're back!" he yelled, racing to open the gate.

Jake drove the car right up to the front door and switched off the lights. Anna came hurrying around the corner from the shadows.

"What happened?" she asked, excitedly.

"Let's go inside first," said her father, firmly.

"But—" began Harry, riding up and braking with a loud screech, as he saw the boys climbing sleepily out of the back of the car.

"Put your bike away now," said his father sternly. "Everyone inside, and please shut the door before we turn on any lights."

They all hurried into the cool, dark hall. Apart from a slight ripple on the water surface, the goldfish were invisible in the pond. The dog's tail was beating rhythmically on the banisters. Jake shut the door and Anna turned on a lamp which diffused a pale light over the room. There were no curtains at the windows as the house was not overlooked, and the long drive gave privacy from the lane.

It was only when they were all seated and Jake wanted to introduce the little boys that they realized that they did not know their names. Jake pulled out their passports. Guy François was five years old, they discovered, and Pierre Louis seven. As they were both so slight, they appeared younger. Jake smiled at them as he read out their names, but they only stared back solemnly. But they were each clutching a purring cat.

"Oh no, I wonder if that's what they are called?"

Anna and Harry looked questioningly at their parents, waiting for an explanation. Meg quickly told them what had happened. Anna smiled to herself and her mother looked at her quizzically.

"Oh Mum, I was just thinking that every time you leave the house, you come back with more and more people and animals. It'll have to stop or we'll be bursting at the seams."

Her mother laughed. "Not to worry. I also have to tell you that we are taking the train to Bangkok tomorrow and will continue on to the beach in Pattaya."

"Great," said Harry. "But we'll need a private train for us all."

"Steady on, Harry," said Jake. "It's just the boys and you three."

"But Dad, what about Lian's girls? They'd love the beach. And aren't you coming?"

"Lian and the girls will stay here, and I'll come later, once I've found Louis."

"That's enough," said Meg, standing up briskly. "Let's get organized for the night." While Anna went to check on Lian's girls, Meg shepherded the boys and their cats upstairs.

Harry helped Meg transfer his bed for them and unfolded a camp bed for himself, grumbling under his breath. Meg smiled to herself, as she rummaged in Harry's cupboard for some pyjamas. Certainly their family was growing by leaps and bounds.

Guy and Pierre undressed and washed without a sound, and although they refused cookies, they drank the juice Anna brought upstairs for them. Once finished, they climbed silently into bed and the cats stretched out contentedly at their feet. Meg tucked them in with a friendly smile and left the door ajar so light would filter in.

Meg sat down with a sigh beside her husband on the couch, and he silently handed her a strong cup of tea, which she accepted gratefully. Harry came and joined them a little later.

"Well, how are we going to do this?" Meg asked, taking a long sip. She was worried. It appeared simple enough to take the ferry across to Thailand and go to the seaside for a few weeks. But before that they would have to pass the Lao security check and have their passports stamped.

"I know that their passports are in order, but what if they are looking out for them and refuse to let them go?"

Jake patted her shoulder and said gruffly, "As you say, their passports are in order, and they have the correct visas. Nothing should go wrong. If the communists are waiting to stop them, that will be out of your control." He smiled. "I must say, those guys at my briefing in Ottawa, when I got the job, had no idea of conditions in the field. It all seemed so cut, dried and organized when they were explaining my role here. Real life is so much more complicated, a far cry from the theory."

Meg laughed ruefully, as she poured out second cups. "My dear, it only confirms what you have always said: the bureaucrats in Ottawa have no idea of all the problems that beset our lives in the field; or they make sure not to know about these problems.

"I was amazed at those little boys. They didn't utter a word or show in the slightest way how they were feeling. The inscrutable face of Asia. If our two had been in a similar situation at that age, they would have howled and probably have had to be dragged away from me."

"Oh Mum, they're probably scared to death," Harry said. "Imagine how they must feel to suddenly find themselves in the hands of huge foreign devils. I expect once we're on the beach, they'll relax a bit and be regular kids."

"Yes, you're probably right, Harry. Now I think we should all go to bed. We'll pack in the morning and cross over before lunch."

"But the train doesn't go until the evening, Mum. What on earth will we do for a whole afternoon and evening in Nongkhai?" groaned Anna, coming in from the kitchen. She held a large sandwich in her hands, "I was hungry," she explained. "Lian came home, by the way."

"I know Nongkhai isn't the most exciting place to be, but I would rather cross when it's busy in the morning. I feel we'll be less visible. We'll be able to have a leisurely lunch and we must buy some clothes for the boys. Because, as you probably didn't notice, they only have what they arrived in. We can then have supper before getting on the train—and since we'll be exhausted by then, we should sleep soundly all the way to Bangkok. Don't you agree, Jake?"

"It's your decision, Meg. I don't know whether such an early crossing for the night train is absolutely essential, but I'll drive you all to the ferry."

"Will it take you long to find Louis, Dad?"

"I have no idea. But until you're all safely in Pattaya, I have no intention of stirring anything up. I may be lucky and find him straight away, or there may not be a whisper. It depends on many things—especially Michel Lee."

"Do be careful, Jake. Whatever Ottawa told you, you know we should not meddle in internal affairs, you don't want to end up in prison as well."

"I'll be very cautious, I can assure you. I know one or two people who might be able to help, but I have no intention of crossing Michel Lee's path—he could be very dangerous.

However, I feel obliged to help this man who has been working for Canada all these years. Now he's in danger, we cannot abandon him or his family. I also feel we owe it to Père
Gregoire. He loved this country so much and look at it now.
My instructions did not cover this eventuality, but we are all
going to do our best for them. Let's just hope we can reunite
them in freedom, and that it's not already too late.''

15

The Plot Thickens

They were up early the next morning. Lian had gently coaxed a few words out of the little boys and was able to confirm that they were indeed called Guy and Pierre. Lian was upset to learn that the Porters, except for Jake, were leaving for Thailand. Life had become very frightening and strange, and she had received no word from her husband. She felt safe with the family around her, but once they were gone she would feel vulnerable and unprotected. Still, Jake would be staying awhile, and she just hoped they'd not be away too long.

They took little luggage with them and crossed the frontier without a problem. Jake cheerily waved goodbye from the bank as the ferry slowly puttered across the river to Nongkhai.

By the evening, they were all weary and footsore, from walking and shopping and simply waiting around in the little town, and they gladly rode to the train in two samlaws in the gathering dusk. On the way loud music poured over the narrow streets from the shops and cafes along the way.

Guy and Pierre had never been on a train before, let alone

slept on one, and they bounced up and down on the bunks once the kindly attendant had made them up.

As they all went off to sleep, lulled by the rocking motion of the train as it rumbled through the flat countryside to Bangkok, they were unaware that Michel had also left Vientiane. He had crossed over by ferry in the late afternoon, and was now on his way by overnight bus to Bangkok.

At dawn the train slowly shuddered to a halt in Bangkok. The city was still not fully awake at that hour. The streets were being hosed down and swept, a few taxis and cars were hurtling wildly along, and yawning shopkeepers were stretching and hawking as they opened their stores. Little food stalls were being set up on street corners, and the bars and nightclubs were closing.

By early afternoon, they were at the beach hotel at Pattaya. The bus ride had been rapid and comfortable, and the few additional miles in a brightly decorated open taxi had been exhilarating in the bright sunshine, their hair blowing about their faces.

Their three-bedroomed cabin was on the very edge of the white sand of the beach. They quickly changed and ran down to the sea. When they'd had enough of the water, Harry and Anna built a sand castle for Guy and Pierre, who took turns running back and forth collecting water to fill the moat.

By late afternoon, the sun quickly dipped behind the tall palms along the curve of the beach, and dusk came swiftly. The night was velvety warm and the water looked dark and smooth.

At dinner time they strolled up the steep path to the little restaurant. They sat under a palm-thatch roof on the verandah, which was strung with coloured lights, and ate freshly caught fish and juicy pineapple.

Some other guests were laughing and chatting in the bar, and a few dogs cautiously watched from the shadows, but a cat came up boldly demanding food.

"Poor Dad, still stuck in Vientiane," remarked Harry, pushing back his empty plate. "I hope we can stay here for ages."

"I expect we will," replied Meg, contentedly. "It may take your father quite a while, and once he arrives here he'll need a good rest."

"Lovely," sighed Anna.

*

In Bangkok, Michel was sitting in the backroom of a pharmacist's shop. The elderly pharmacist, perched on a stool beside him, felt uneasy and annoyed at his intrusion. He twisted a small glass of tea in his hands.

"I don't know what you expect of me, Michel," he growled. "François is my friend, our political thinking is similar—we are not crazy like you. I don't wish to see my country brought down on its knees, destroyed, taken over by a foreign power as in Laos. I'm loyal to my King, as François is loyal to your poor King—now a powerless prisoner in his own country. Michel, we were friends. Our honoured mothers were like sisters, but until you come to your senses, I can no longer have anything to do with you.

"If I do happen to be in touch with François, I'll tell him about Nurse. May she rest in peace with our ancestors. He'll be greatly distressed, as I am. She was a part of the old, good life you used to enjoy. That she should die amongst strangers, foreigners, is unpardonable. But they must be good people.'' The little man sighed heavily, putting down his glass. ''But you, Michel, are a wicked man. I suppose until your lust for power is satisfied, you and your leader, Souphanouvong—strange, two younger sons—will trample your poor countrymen and your families underfoot.

''Why do you want to see François, I wonder? To gloat at his defeat? Can you not leave him in peace? If he has left Laos, do you think he went gladly? Laos is his country. It will have been with grief and a heavy heart that he'll have turned his back, but he must have realized that after all these years of war, Laos is lost. Let us hope, Michel, that your Communist power will be short-lived, and that François's grandsons will return one day to win back their homeland. That is, if you and your kind leave anything to win back.''

The elderly man stood up, his face dark with anger, his hands shaking as he opened the door into a small back passage. ''Go, go,'' he said.

Michel rose, bowed low to his one-time boyhood friend, and silently left without a word or a backward glance.

François had not left Bangkok. In fact, he was staying with his old friend, Boon. Distressed that his family had not arrived, he delayed his departure to France, day by day. But now at last Boon had news for him. Bad news, but news still. Boon was cautious. For ten minutes after Michel left, he sat quietly in the small backroom until his heart stopped fluttering and his hands shaking.

Then he returned to his shop, where his young assistant

was busy attending to some customers. He remained there until the shutters were put up for the night, and the young assistant had left on his noisy motorbike. Only then did Boon climb the outside stairs to his apartment above, where his wife was busily preparing his supper. His old friend, François Lee, sat quietly nearby with a newspaper in his hands, staring at it with sightless eyes, his thoughts far away. "Ah, Boon."

Boon padded in silently and, once seated, accepted the bowl of soup from his wife.

"Michel came to visit me."

"My brother?"

"Yes, Michel your brother—he wanted news of you. I told him we could no longer be friends. We must be careful."

"I wonder why he is in Bangkok."

"So do I, old friend. Anyway he brought news of your family."

"He did? Tell me."

"It is not good," said Boon slowly, shaking his head.

François leant forward. "Tell me at once," he demanded.

"Your daughter is all right but still in Vientiane, and her husband has been arrested."

"Oh no—and the boys?"

"Your grandsons are in Thailand. They were seen crossing over yesterday with your foreign friends—the woman and children."

"Then they are safe at least," whispered François, softly through his teeth, and nervously cracked the joints of his fingers.

"There is other bad news."

"Yes?"

"Your old nurse is dead. Michel turned her out of the house and she died amongst strangers—these same foreigners took her in."

François sighed. "But what of Mimi? Why did she not leave with her children?"

"No doubt, she intends to secure the release of her husband," said Boon drily. "I think you should go to France immediately. Michel is up to no good, and he has spies everywhere."

"I know. I expect the Canadian will help Mimi as he has stayed behind. I wonder where the children are? I could take them to France with me."

"A woman with four children would be unlikely to remain in Bangkok. I should imagine they'll go to the coast."

"Yes, you're right—no doubt they've gone to Pattaya. Tomorrow I'll go and look for them. Then we can fly directly to my son in Paris. At least my grandsons will be safe and the fate of Mimi and Louis is in the hands of Buddha."

"And this foreigner," muttered Boon.

"Yes, of course," said François, impatiently, "he will find Louis, and as soon as Mimi and he arrive here, you must send them to France, my old friend."

Although Michel had learnt nothing from Boon, he felt that his brother would not have left Thailand. His daughter and grandsons meant too much to him—the sentimental old fool. But the trap had been set. All he had to do now was locate the "felang" woman and the children, and François would come to him. With local help, he would take all three

back to Vientiane and then the felang man would be dealt
with as well. Stupid, interfering fool. He seemed to imagine
himself to be some modern-day Scarlet Pimpernel!

16

Prisoners

Early the next morning, while Meg and the children were on the beach, Michel in Bangkok was impatiently awaiting a phone call from a comrade in Pattaya.

In Vientiane, Jake clambered down from a samlaw and walked quickly along the irregular pavement, shaded by large trees, past several small stores and entered Mr Phong's electrical appliance shop. The Chinese owner hurried to greet him, and they both walked into the back of the store and sat down at his desk.

"The exchange rate is again higher," commented Mr Phong.

"I haven't come to change money today," explained Jake. "I need information." The Chinese nodded without speaking. He was a businessman, and he not only exchanged dollars on the black market for the foreigners who came to him by recommendation, but also helped them in many other ways.

Jake explained about Louis's disappearance. The Chinese was acquainted with him and would see what he could find out. He shook his head sorrowfully, so many people were being picked up, it was becoming dangerous. Soon, possibly in a day or two, he would leave the country. His shop was already sold, at a fair price considering the troubled times, to an Indian, who was gambling on staying a while longer before selling again, probably to a Lao. Phong had money in Thailand and gold and US dollars in his pocket. He and his sons would start from scratch yet again and prosper, until perhaps once more the approaching tide of communism would undermine their fragile roots. He was not so eager to move on now, he was becoming old, but the family must remain together, and he had young grandsons for whom they must build for the future.

"Come back this evening," he told Jake. "By then I should know whether it's possible to get news of him."

Jake was greeted by an excited, incoherent Tee at the gate, and in the house an anxious Lian was trying to calm a hysterical Vivienne Bartlett, one of Meg's English friends. Somphong was crouching in the kitchen doorway and the three little girls sat beneath the table with Beauty and the cats all watching with round eyes.

"Vivienne, what is it?" demanded Jake, wondering how he was going to cope with this new situation. If only Meg had been here.

"Jake, oh Jake," screamed Vivienne, leaping up from her chair and throwing herself at him. "Frank has been arrested. You must find him and have him released."

"Now calm down, Vivienne, and tell me exactly what happened. Lian, please bring some tea."

Lian thankfully hurried out, her children scampering after her, followed by the cats and the dog.

"I have been waiting for hours, and Lian tells me that Meg has gone to Pattaya," she said, accusingly.

"Yes, she and the children left yesterday. Now tell me, Vivienne, what happened."

"Well, you see," began Vivienne, "we met this charming young French couple at the du Croix's luncheon. They have just arrived and need a car. Frank immediately thought of the Greens, who we knew were on the point of leaving and had been unable to sell their car. So Frank drove them round there after work. They rang the bell but there was no answer, and as the gate was unlocked, they just walked in. The house was empty. The Greens must have already left, but the car was still parked outside the house. The two men were looking it over, but the young wife, not interested in cars, wandered off into the garden. The Greens do have a beautiful garden. After about ten minutes, a group of Pathet Lao burst in, bristling with guns, and grabbed Frank and Richard Larocque, tied their hands behind their backs with rope, and hustled them out to a waiting truck. They didn't notice Marie Larocque who, as soon as they had driven off, rushed round to the French Embassy. Luckily someone was still there and they came round to tell me what had happened. But they don't seem to be able to locate our husbands."

"Don't worry, Vivienne, it's just a question of making the rounds of various police cells. I'll find Frank and get him released."

"Oh, I knew you would!"

*

Jake was in luck. The young guards were lounging in the shade and were overawed by the large, hairy felang. They let him walk into the cell block at the back of the police station without any trouble.

The large cells, with bars from ceiling to floor, encircled an open courtyard, and were crowded with men of all ages who'd been rounded up during the night. Fear showed in their eyes, and several dejected youths had their heads shaved, because they'd sported long, decadent "Western hairstyles." There were several foreigners among them, even a priest, and they all crowded at the bars on seeing Jake, asking for messages to be delivered. He quickly wrote down their names, promising to let people know where they were. Frank was not among them.

At the second place it was more difficult to gain entry, but he finally pushed his way in, hoping he'd not be arrested as well. The cells were dirty and little light filtered in through the door but Jake, silhouetted in the doorway, was immediately recognized, and his name was called from two different cells. He found Frank and Louis, both looking battered and exhausted.

"Goodness, a jackpot," exclaimed Jake.

The other prisoners watched enviously as a jubilant Frank, in a torn shirt, bellowed at Jake.

"I knew I could rely on you, old chap." Turning, he pointed at a pale young man leaning against the filthy wall, with one eye painfully closed and swollen. "He's in pretty bad shape—they were a bit rough."

Louis Sombat stood pressed against the bars, silent and calm. "Alright," said Jake. "I know where you are now. I'll inform the embassies straight away and they'll deal with you and your colleague, Frank. Louis is another matter. I'll be back as quickly as possible."

The British and French embassies were relieved to hear that their citizens had been found and immediately set the correct wheels in motion for their release. Jake rushed to the old wooden house by the river where Louis's wife Mimi was staying with her great-aunt.

He left the car at the side of the main road between browsing buffalo and hurried down the narrow pathway to the large, dilapidated house.

Jake knocked at the door. No one came. He muttered impatiently and shuffled his feet in the dust. He was just about to knock again, when the door opened a crack. A pale, frightened face peered out.

"Mimi," cried Jake.

"Shsh," she warned, putting a finger to her lips, and quickly opened the door just wide enough to let Jake in. "You gave me such a fright, banging on the door like that."

"I'm sorry," said Jake contritely, "it's just that I've found Louis. You must be prepared to leave tonight."

"Oh, thank you." She pressed her lips tightly together in relief, tears pricking her eyes, and then hurried into the back of the house calling her aunt. She came back almost at once, with a tiny, smooth-faced old lady who nodded and bowed repeatedly before the huge, loud foreigner.

"My great-aunt,"

"Will she come too?"

Mimi shook her head. "No, she says she's too old to leave her home, but she knows that Louis and I must go. I will be waiting for you."

"Bring nothing, only your papers, no suitcases."

*

Phong looked at Jake in alarm, as he stormed into the shop, and came forward hurriedly, with a worried frown. He indicated with a nod his two young assistants who were serving customers—they were not family, and therefore not to be trusted. Jake looked around desperately for an idea.

"A lamp. I'm interested in buying a lamp," he said, noticing some lamps in an unattended corner. Mr Phong quickly led him over to them, and demonstrated their good points.

"I've found him," said Jake.

"Good," said the Chinese, "I wondered why you had returned so soon."

"I'll need a boat tonight."

"I'll see what I can do, but it is more and more difficult and they are demanding high prices."

"That doesn't matter," said Jake.

"How many?"

"Two."

"Alright, I think it can be arranged. Please be on the river bank below the Russian Embassy at nine."

"Isn't that a bit public?"

"Yes, the guards are busy watching the Embassy, so they are careless about the river. There are numerous garden plots and small huts on the bank. You'll have to be careful in the dark, the path is steep and very narrow. No lights, no ciga-

rettes and no luggage. Bring US cash. This should be suffi-
cient,'' and Phong wrote an amount on the palm of his hand
and then quickly rubbed it off with his other hand.

"Your friends will be leaving with my family."

Jake nodded, bowed slightly, and hurried out of the shop.

17

A Bribe

The two embassy cars, a Bentley and a Renault, came to a halt before the police station. The chauffeurs jumped out to open the passengers' doors. A middle-aged florid-faced Englishman stepped down from the first, and greeted his French opposite number—an older, lean, and remote-looking man. Together they moved to the door, where the teenage guards had suddenly become alert and were eyeing them suspiciously.

A jeep approached, rattled to a halt and a Lao government officer, a large man in a drab grey uniform, hoisted himself out. Jake brought up the rear in his family car. He passed the other vehicles parked across from the entrance and carefully backed up right outside the door. He left both front doors of his car slightly open so that he and Louis, whom he intended to "liberate," could easily get in quickly.

The four men bowed to each other and the officer led the way in. The young guards stood at attention. An older guard sat at a table just inside the door. The officer spoke to him briskly, handing him some documents.

The guard squinted at the documents, verifying the contents, as he read each word, using his finger as a guide. Once he was satisfied, he pulled out a stamp and ink pad and stamped each sheet, seemingly oblivious of the numerous eyes watching him. He calmly signed each copy and then filed them into different folders, handing back a yellow copy to the officer. Only then did he stand up and unlock the first cell.

Frank stepped out slowly leading a dazed Richard Larocque. The two embassy officials moved quickly to help, the older man angrily addressing the officer regarding the treatment of the two men, but the officer merely ignored his protests, nodding at the guard as he turned and walked out.

Jake hung back close to the bars of Louis' cell. He spoke to Louis in a loud-voiced whisper and passed him a brown paper bag. The guard leapt forward and grabbed it angrily. He looked inside and gasped at the sight of so much money. Louis spoke quietly and firmly, telling him that if he opened the door the money was his. The guard looked from one man to the other, and then to the front door. The others had left. There was the sound of the jeep moving away, and the bang of car doors. Stuffing the bag down the front of his baggy jacket, the guard opened the cell door.

Without a word, Jake hurried out with Louis and they were in his car and following discreetly behind the Bentley ahead in a matter of seconds. Louis lay on the floor covered with a rug.

"We'll go to my friend's house for now, and tonight you cross over to Thailand with your wife," Jake told Louis

"And my sons?"

"They are already in Thailand with my family."

Louis let out a sigh of relief. "Thank you," he said.

Jake nodded, his hands tightly clenching the wheel. He glanced in the rear mirror, but no one seemed to be following. The car drew up inside the British Embassy grounds and with a quick word to Louis to stay put, Jake quickly caught up with the other men on the steps.

"I'll take Frank home now."

"Straight away? I thought we might discuss this over a cup of tea," said the Englishman, in surprise. His name was Masters. "They have both been given twenty-four hours to leave, you know."

Jake quickly reflected on the problems ahead. "Okay, I'll cross over with Frank and Vivienne tomorrow, as I'm going to join my family at the beach. It would be a good idea for them to join us. They'll need to relax after this ordeal and reflect on their future. When Meg and I return, we can arrange to ship their things to them. In the meantime, their staff can look after the house for another month. What do you say, Frank?"

"Sounds fine to me," replied easygoing Frank.

"Good, let's go. Vivienne is hysterical and the sooner you're home the better."

"Just a minute," said Masters.

"Yes, well do you agree?" asked Jake impatiently.

"Yes, seems good enough. You realize that they were charged with spying—the house has been requisitioned by the Pathet Lao." Turning to Frank, he continued, "I will come over this evening with all the documents. You must also compose a telegram to your head office and we can send it away from here."

"Thanks, Masters, thanks for everything," Frank replied. "First time I've been behind bars and not a situation I would like to repeat." He turned to face the pale young Frenchman, who had been in jail with him and had now found a door jamb on which he could lean. "Goodbye then, Richard. Sorry we made your stay in the country so short, but just one of those things, I'm afraid."

"Ne vous faites pas, Frank, I'm just so glad your friend was 'ere to find us. My thanks, Jake, I could not 'ave supported more," said the Frenchman, emotionally kissing them both on each cheek. "Per'aps we'll meet again one day in Paris."

Frank and Jake went down to the car, and the others moved out of sight into the Embassy.

"Sorry to rush you away like this, Frank," apologized Jake, "but I sprung Louis unofficially at the same time." Jake quickly introduced the two men as he started the engine.

Once he was sure they were not being followed, he relaxed slightly and explained, "Louis and his wife have to leave tonight. Louis will have to stay with you while I collect Mimi. We'll all meet in Bangkok and go together to join Meg and the kids. Louis' two are with Meg."

"I can see you're up to your eyeballs in intrigue," said Frank with a big grin.

"Quite unintentionally," said Jake, ruefully, "but so many of my friends need to be sprung from jail."

*

The car crept along the narrow road without lights. The night was dark and silent as it was already an hour past curfew. So far they had been lucky and had kept clear of patrols and roadblocks on the small back roads.

Louis and Mimi sat straight and tense in the back. Jake's hands were damp on the wheel, as he slowly edged the car around the next corner. Still nothing. The lane was deserted, and the only sound was a dog whining near by. He quietly parked the car under a high wall and cut the engine. Without turning, he said, "safer to walk from here as we have to cross the main road which is illuminated. It could be tricky. Come on, let's go."

Walking calmly and slowly, they crossed the road, clearly visible in the bright light, but they reached the shadows on the other side without incident.

"They must have been looking the other way," said Jake.

Mimi giggled nervously. Carefully, one behind the other, they descended a narrow, steep ravine which led down to the river. It was filled with garbage and they could hear rats scurrying away as they approached. It was dark away from the road, as there was no moon and the trees were dense. They inched their way cautiously down, a can scrapped against a stone, the long grass swished around their legs, and their feet squelched in the rotten mess. The smell was bad. Finally, coming out from the undergrowth, Jake found a tiny path which led through neatly cultivated patches of vegetables, which they could just discern in the darkness.

The water was darker than the night. A few lights twinkled across the river in Thailand, and there were other lights on a small island downstream where there was a Pathet Lao post. Jake looked at his watch. It was already eight-thirty. He wondered how much further they should go. Trees hid the road so he could not see where the Russian Embassy was situated.

Suddenly a figure loomed up in front of them, making Mimi gasp in fear. It was Phong. He beckoned them to follow. They crossed a ditch on a narrow plank and scrambled down a steep incline to a small hut—a black square in the darkness. Crouched before it, at the edge of the river, was a crowd of people.

"My family," whispered Phong. There were also large bundles, boxes tied with string and baskets—the Chinese family was not leaving empty handed.

At a word from Phong, his sons silently started to load the luggage onto the long, narrow boat. By the time it was all stowed aboard there did not seem much room for passengers. But the sons quickly shepherded their mother, their wives, numerous children and babies on board, where they perched on and among the luggage. Phong motioned to Louis and Mimi to follow suit. Jake handed him the dollars in a packet and the Chinese passed it to his eldest son. Not a baby cried, not a sound was made except for the gentle lapping of the water against the sides of the boat as it settled deeper in the water. The four sons had short paddles. Jake and Phong waded into the water to push the boat clear, and within a few moments it had vanished into the darkness on its way to Nongkhai.

"You're not leaving?" Jake asked Phong.

"Very soon. Tomorrow or the next day. I shall go legally across the border on a business trip."

They waited, squatting down before the hut until they heard the motor starting in the distance. Nothing stirred around them.

"Good," said Phong. "I shall go now. Give me twenty minutes before you come."

"Thank you," said Jake, as the Chinese bowed and vanished into the darkness.

Half an hour later, just as Jake was about to follow, there was the sound of shots from the direction of the road and then all was quiet again.

"Blast," said Jake, wondering if Phong was all right. He decided to spend the night where he was and hoped the mosquitoes would leave him alone.

18

Kidnapped

Harry was woken by the creak of the screen door. It was still dark outside. He slipped out of bed and looked out of the window. François Lee was walking barefooted through the sand to the water's edge. He hunkered down and gazed out to sea. The sun was rising and the water lapped contentedly up the white sand and over his feet. He didn't move—he was obviously contented.

Harry went back to bed and remembered the sudden appearance yesterday of Mr Lee. He had come walking down the beach, and Pierre and Guy had rushed him, shouting, laughing and crying all at once. They had stood hugging each other for the longest time. Harry was glad for them, and also pretty envious, as his own Granddad was thousands of miles away.

At suppertime, Mr Lee had told them that he had absolute confidence that Jake would rescue Louis. All he had to do was enjoy the sea with his grandsons until Louis and Mimi joined them and they would leave for France together. Harry hoped that this prediction would come true.

An hour or so later, he was woken by Pierre and Guy

bouncing on his bed, demanding he wake up and go swimming with them. Anna and Meg were already in the water, and the boys ran headlong in to join them. They all loved this carefree time at the beach when they were able to live in their swimwear all day long, and no one grumbled if they tracked sand into the cabin.

Meg and Anna went to prepare breakfast, leaving the boys to cavort in the water, watched over dotingly by Mr Lee. But they all responded immediately when Meg called them from the cabin. The little boys had regained their appetites and their faces glowed, now their beloved grandfather was with them.

They were all sitting around the kitchen table eating scrambled eggs when, without any warning, the kitchen door burst open and three armed men rushed in. They all sat quite still for a moment as it was such a shock. Then there was a clatter of cutlery on plates. Anna choked on a mouthful of tea, and Harry jumped up, "Hey, what gives?"

"Naang loong, naang long," cried the first man, commanding them to sit down, as both Meg and Mr Lee pushed back their chairs to stand up. Neither of the little boys moved as they cowered in their chairs.

Only then did Michel enter the room with a grim, satisfied smile on his face. Ignoring his brother François and Meg, he told Guy and Pierre, "Yun keun (Get up), ma ne (come here)." They glanced at their grandfather.

"Ma ne," snarled Michel at them, and they hurriedly slipped off their chairs and slowly walked over to him. He spun them around and grasped them by their shoulders, making them wince with pain. "You too, François, must come."

"No, never," cried François.

"Do you want me to kill your grandsons?"

François stood up, glaring with hatred at his brother.

"I will come, but let the boys stay here."

"Oh no, you're all needed."

"Needed? Where?"

"In Vientiane—where you belong, not among the felang."

Two of the men hustled the three prisoners out of the cottage, holding a pistol at François's back.

Michel bowed mockingly at Meg. "Stop interfering, Madam. Forget my brother and his grandsons. My man will remain with you until we are safely back on Lao soil." With a nod at the armed man at the door, he hurried after the others.

"Mother, do something!"

Meg looked at her daughter helplessly, "*What* can I do, Anna?"

19

Panic

Just before dawn, when the birds began chirping, Jake stood up and stretched. He felt chilled through and he ached all over. He carefully made his way to the road and was glad to find people were already on their way to market. His car started without difficulty and he drove home. Lian was distraught, as she'd waited up for him all night and, as time passed, had imagined a variety of terrible things happening to him. She scolded him sharply and sent him off to have a hot shower, while she prepared his breakfast.

An hour or so later, he felt much better as he drove to the Bartlett's house. He found Vivienne running from one bulging suitcase to another, not accomplishing very much. Frank had taken refuge in his study, where he was emptying his desk drawers of papers and sorting them into two piles. The first was being burned by his gardener outside and the other he was packing.

"Hello, we're almost ready. I've decided its safer to take my papers along. Spies can't leave incriminating documents lying around," and he gave a short mocking laugh. "How about some coffee before we start?" Jake nodded in agreement. The good effects from his shower and breakfast were swiftly wearing off. He felt unbelievably tired, and coffee would help to keep him awake. Frank heaved himself up from the desk, and opening the door he bellowed, "Mey, Mey, bring some coffee please."

Returning to his sorting, he remarked, "The house is in turmoil. Mey is very upset, but she's promised to stay till you return. My God, I never thought this would happen to us, you now, yes—always meddling . . . "

"Steady on, Frank, I don't meddle. I try to mind my own business and get on with my own affairs, but people will come to me. I can't refuse to help—someone must help."

"I apologize. You're right and your help is much appreciated. But do be careful, Jake. All I can say, is thank God you found us in that stinking hole. But Jake, what if it should happen to you, who will get *you* out?"

Jake's plan was to cross over on the car ferry with Frank and Vivienne to Nongkhai. Then they would drive to Bangkok—a day's drive—where they would meet up with Louis and Mimi and all go to the beach at Pattaya.

The frontier proceedings were slow and trying. Their suitcases were opened and the car searched. Both Frank and Vivienne were depressed. Mey, their housekeeper, had clung to Vivienne, tears pouring down her face, while her two teenage sons had stood in stony-faced gloom. They were resigned to an unknown future, which was seemingly no longer in the hands of Buddha but in those of the Pathet Lao and the Vietnamese—they would probably be conscripted.

It was lunchtime by the time the car ferry reached the further bank and they were unloaded. They lunched in the

same restaurant where Meg and the children had eaten, gazing across the fast-flowing Mekong to the green banks and
palms of Laos.

"It's strange," commented Vivienne. "Last week, when
so many of our friends were leaving, I also wanted to go, but
now we've had to leave, I want to go back."

"Well, that's impossible, dear. We'll give Jake some more
money for Mey. I expect she'll be quite happy with her
sister."

"But the boys—"

"Vivienne, they are adults. They'll be much better in the
army, keeping out of trouble. Now stop worrying. There is
nothing more we can do, but perhaps Jake will see them
from time to time." Frank turned ruefully to his friend—
"Sorry, Jake, we are loading you with another family."

"And you said I meddled?"

Jake and Frank took turns at the wheel. There were several
roadblocks on the road to Bangkok. This was to keep unde-
sirables out as well as to protect travellers from bandits. The
process of checking papers slowed traffic considerably, so it
was past midnight before they reached the city—too late to
ring Meg or to find out if Louis and Mimi had arrived.

*

Meanwhile in Pattaya, Meg, Anna and Harry dozed uneasily
on the top of the big bed in the main bedroom. The armed
intruder watched them through the open door from the living
room. They had spent the whole day in the living room, and
had only been allowed to move into the kitchen while Meg

prepared food, under his unfriendly stare. He wouldn't let them speak.

Early next morning, Jake put through a call to the cottages. The owner, Xiang, answered the phone. Yes, if Jake would hold on, he would run to fetch Meg. No need, said Jake, he could just give her a message that he would be with them by lunchtime, with the little boys' parents. They would be needing another cottage too, as there were . . .

"But the little boys are no longer here. They left with their grandfather and three other men yesterday."

"Their grandfather was there?"

"Yes, he arrived the day before. He was so happy to be with his grandsons. He just loved the beach and the sea."

"Why did they leave?"

"I don't know. He didn't even say goodbye. Four men arrived in a van and they all left in a great hurry except one . . . One of the men must have stayed behind."

"Stayed behind?" yelled Jake.

"Yes."

"And my family?" asked Jake, very quietly. "Did you speak to my wife yesterday?"

"No, I didn't see her or the children."

"Xiang, please go to the cottage and speak to my wife. But don't insist if a man comes to the door. Just come back and tell me. I'll hold."

"Yes, I'll go quickly," said Xiang sounding thoroughly alarmed. He laid down the phone and ran, as fast as his sandals would allow, down the stone steps to the cottage. He knocked on the door and it opened immediately. The tall guard scowled at him, "Yes?"

"I wish to speak with Madam."

"She's asleep."

"But—"

"She's asleep," and the door was firmly shut in his face.

"It is bad," Xiang panted down the phone to Jake. "I only see the man. He was very unfriendly and said your wife was asleep."

"Was he armed?"

"I don't know. I didn't see a gun, but he was very large and very ugly."

"Now listen," said Jake. "Call the police and tell them my family are being held against their will, and that yesterday an elderly man and his two grandsons were taken by force. I will come as quickly as possible." Jake banged down the phone and hurried to waken Frank and Vivienne.

"Frank, open up," he growled, at the door. Frank opened the door quickly.

"We are almost ready," he said in surprise, as Jake barged into the room and viciously closed the door behind him. He paced up and down nervously as he spoke.

"We're in a heap of trouble," he began, and explained what had happened. "I'll go straight to Pattaya. Frank, you must collect Louis at this address." Jake handed Frank the address scribbled on a piece of paper. "It's a drugstore—and with whatever reinforcements he can muster, make a dash to Nongkhai. They've probably crossed already, so wait for me there. Under no circumstances must either of you cross back to Laos. I'll bring Meg and the children back to Vivienne here and continue on to join you." He rushed out of the room before either Vivienne or Frank could reply.

20

Police Rescue

Xiang immediately phoned the police. The sergeant she met was scornful at first. Was Xiang sure? Of course, Xiang was sure. The people involved were from Laos. This convinced the sergeant, who immediately became businesslike and barked some instructions to Xiang. The other cottages were to be evacuated one by one, with no fuss or panic, so the man in the Porters' cottage would not be warned. It was essential that all the people gather in the bar, and no one must be on the beach or around the cottages. The police would be coming in fast, and they wanted no one in the way, was that clear?

The two armoured trucks rolled in quietly and came to a halt. Two dozen helmeted police jumped out, bristling with equipment. The officer-in-charge came to speak to Xiang who pointed out the cottage. The people in the bar jockeyed for positions by the windows as the men were deployed. The officer spoke through a loudhailer, first in English, "Mrs Porter, this is the police. Please lie on the floor with your children, well away from windows." Then in Thai, he ordered the man to come out with his hands up.

In the cottage, they were all taken completely by surprise as they sat in the kitchen watching Meg prepare breakfast. They froze at the sound of the voice. The guard motioned them to keep still and cautiously looked through the glass kitchen door. They all made note of the armed policemen watching from behind nearby cottages and trees. They waited.

"You have ten seconds."

The guard aimed his pistol at the nearest policeman and fired. With his attention diverted, Meg beckoned Anna and Harry to follow her, and they rushed into the nearest bedroom and banged the door shut. It had no lock, but they put a chair under the handle.

"Quick, into the bathroom," urged Meg, "there are no windows and there's a lock." The lock was flimsy, but still . . .

Shots were fired, there was the sound of running feet outside and a screen door squeaked. More shots, a sharp cry and then silence.

"You may come out now, Mrs Porter," the voice on the loudhailer called. "We have our man."

*

When Jake arrived everything was back to normal. Xiang was working on his books in the office, the cats and dogs slept in the shade, a gardener was slowly sweeping the path, and Jake's family were relaxing on the beach. He hurried down and hugged them with relief.

"Who could have imagined that this could happen?" queried Meg. "If we'd had an inkling, we would have taken some precautions."

"It's not your fault," reassured Jake, "none of us thought that once they had left, Michel would try to get them back. Anyway, Frank and Louis have rushed to Nongkhai, and Vivienne is waiting in Bangkok."

"Vivienne in Bangkok?"

"It's a long story," chuckled Jake. "Come on let's eat, I'm starving. Then I'll tell you the latest news from Vientiane— you're not the only people with exciting lives!"

It was decided that they would return to Vientiane, since they were too upset about the kidnappings to stay on at the beach. Once all the troubles were over, they would return for a long, peaceful vacation. So with only a brief stop in Bangkok to explain what was happening to Vivienne, they continued on to Nongkhai, Jake and Meg taking turns to drive.

In the early hours of the morning, they reached Nongkhai feeling scruffy and very hungry. People were already bustling about in the market, so they sat down at a small stall to eat a Chinese breakfast by the light of flickering candles.

At six, they decided that they could now disturb Frank and Louis. Both men looked haggard. They had not arrived in time yesterday. François, Guy and Pierre had been seen to cross with the first ferry, accompanied by Michel and the escort.

They decided that Frank and Louis should return to their wives in Bangkok, while the Porters would return home so Jake could try to locate François Lee and the boys.

21

The Chinese and French Connections

When they got back, there were two Pathet Lao soldiers stationed at the gate outside their house.

"I'm so glad you're back," cried Lian. "I don't know what's happening, but the two PLs hve been at the gate since dawn. Somphong wouldn't pass them to go to the market, so Tee had to go instead—he was very cross." Lian chatted away as they unpacked the car as quickly as possible, so they could get inside, away from the curious soldiers.

Anna and Harry went to check up on Beauty, the cats, and the rabbits. They were all fine and eager for attention. After they'd made a fuss of them all, Anna went to see the little girls, so Harry went looking for Tee. Tee was feeling out of sorts. He was hot and tired after cycling to the market for the day's food. Harry found him among some seedlings, "watching them grow." He quickly became more alert when Harry began to tell him what had happened at the beach. They were interrupted by Jake calling everyone to a meeting.

Over hot tea, the Porters told Lian, Somphong and Tee what had happened in Thailand.

"Those poor little boys."

"Yes, they're having a really tough time. I now have to find them. But you people have to decide whether you want to stay working here or not. We don't want you to go but, under the circumstances . . . "

"We stay."

"But Lian, consider a moment. You have your daughters to think of as well.

"I know, I know. We will stay. So will Tee and Somphong. Won't you?" she asked sharply. Tee nodded in agreement and Somphong giggled nervously. "See, we'll all stay. End of conversation."

*

Jake drove straight to the British Embassy where he dropped off Anna and Harry at the pool. Then he hurried inside to speak to Masters.

"Hello," said Masters, looking up from his desk, "that was a very brief holiday. No problems, I hope?"

"Plenty of problems," said Jake, sitting down wearily, "but it's best you don't know the details. We left Frank and Vivienne in Bangkok, and they're fine. I'm going to be sticking my neck out a bit in the next few days, so should my wife come to say I've disappeared—will you please search for me?"

"Well really, Porter, I don't think that's advisable. I think you should just get on with your work, you know. Don't involve yourself in anything else. Frank and Richard were very lucky."

"I know. But I have to finish this one thing. Then my

family and I will sit back and mind our own business. As long as we're not deported."

"I don't know why you haven't been already."

"Thanks. Anyway, I must get along. I'm going to borrow Frank's car for a bit—it may give me half-an-hour's privacy. We acquired a couple of Pathet Lao at our gate, this morning."

"You did? That's bad. Do watch out, Jake, old chap. Here's the car key—the car was just where Frank had left it. The tank is half full—you can settle with me for that."

The Lees' house looked deserted when Jake drove past by it ten minutes later. He quietly turned the car at the end of the lane and parked beside the Medlicott's old house. The gardener came hurrying to the gate and let Jake in. They went round to the back of the house, out of sight, and sat down on the back step.

Jake briefly explained to the gardener what had happened. The young man had noticed nothing unusual down the lane, but he and his family were keeping as quiet as possible, since they did not want trouble. If he noticed anything he would leave a message at the Embassy. But he did not want to become involved and asked Jake not to return. It was not wise to be seen talking to foreigners.

Jake returned the car to the embassy, but pocketed the car key for another time. He drove off in his own car to the town centre.

There was a turbaned Indian sitting on a stool at the door of Phong's electrical shop.

"Good morning," said Jake, "I see the Phongs have left."

"Yes, all except for the old man. He was shot and is in hospital."

Poor old Phong, thought Jake. I'd better pay him a visit.
We may be able to help each other.

The hospital was so overcrowded that the patients were
lying on the corridor floors, leaving only just enough space
for a narrow path to walk through. Most of the patients lay
with their faces turned to the wall, stoically silent and alone
in their pain and misery.

Phong shared a room with three other elderly men. He
was in a bad way. His skin was grey and his eyes were dull,
but he brightened perceptibly on seeing Jake. Jake gave him
a bag of mangoes he'd bought at the hospital entrance.

"I'm surprised to find you here, old friend."

Phong smiled ruefully, "I'm an old fool. They saw me and
look where I am. But it could be worse. In another day or
two I will join my family."

"Good, I'm glad. But I have more problems . . ." Jake
began and explained what had happened.

"You would like me to make inquiries?"

"You could?"

"Anything is possible for American dollars."

"Of course."

"Come back tomorrow at the same time and bring me
some food—I must build up my strength. A bottle of whisky
could be useful, as well."

Jake was greatly relieved. Phong, even laid up in his hospital bed, was confident he'd get news of Lee and the boys.
It was becoming expensive, but what were a few dollars,
some food and a bottle of whisky compared with three lives?

*

The next day, Jake arrived at the hospital early. He had brought soup in a Thermos, some of Lian's cold chicken and rice, and a large bottle of whisky. Phong was sitting up in bed looking much better. Jake sat down on the edge of the bed and Phong quickly drank the soup. Jake waited patiently. Phong started chewing at a chicken leg, grunting with pleasure, wiping his greasy fingers on his soiled pyjamas.

"Your friends are in an aunt's house by the river. They are well guarded. I don't know how you'll get a message to them, let alone rescue them. I cannot help any more, I'm afraid, as I am leaving tonight. You have many enemies, my friend, be very careful," he cautioned. "The old aunt will have to leave too. She is terrified of Michel Lee and so cannot be trusted, she would blabber in her fear within seconds. They are near the airport so you might have more of a chance flying out than going across the river." Phong scrapped up the last grains of rice and leaned back with a contented sigh. "Thank you."

"Thank you for your help, Phong. You are probably right. Use the whisky well and safe journey."

At the gate, Jake was stopped by an earnest young woman with short, straight black hair framing her face and black metal spectacles perched on her nose. She was dressed in a dark blue Mao suit. Although Jake recognized her as a member of the Chinese embassy, he had never met her but she seemed to know him.

"Mr Porter, how fortunate to bump into you."

Jake bowed politely. She came very close and standing on tiptoes, peered up at him.

"I would like to say, on behalf of my people, how very

much we appreciated your help with regard young Dr Louis Sombat. Such a talented man. Now we will be able to look forward to his continued dedicated work in Canada," and she gave Jake a small mischievous smile. "As you are leaving soon, we would like you to accept this small token, and she pressed a small red book into his hand. With a brief nod, she scurried away into the crowd. Jake stared after her in surprise, as he was left clutching a copy of Chairman Mao's quotations.

"So you see," said Jake, sometime later, to his family. "Phong believes we should fly them out."

"But they can't just get on a plane," exclaimed Meg.

"Mother," said Anna in exasperation, "of course not. They need to be flown out in a little four-seater from the Flying Club."

"Yes, but who do we know who flies and would risk being shot down?" demanded Meg.

"It's a lot to ask," agreed Jake.

"But lots of people would do it for dollars," said Anna cynically.

"I have a contact," said Harry

"You do?"

"Sure, that Frenchman with the beard who eats in our little restaurant. We had a long chat one day, and he mentioned that he flies at the Club."

"I doubt whether he'd be willing to smuggle people out."

"No, I'm sure he wouldn't, but he might know someone who would."

"Good thinking, Harry. Let's go and have lunch."

"But lunch is ready here," protested Meg.

"We can eat it this evening."

The Frenchman was drinking his coffee and smoking a strong Gaulloise. Jake decided to take the plunge immediately.

"I believe you fly at the Club?"

"Yes. However, it's becoming more difficult with the lack of fuel. But I adore it."

"Do many people still fly?"

"Regrettably only a handful, and all foreigners. The locals can't afford it any more, although quite a few veterans come by, hoping for a free ride."

"They do? We're looking for a plane and a pilot to the US base in Udon. Do you know of anyone?"

The Frenchman raised an eyebrow and frowned. "A bit risky," he stated finally. "But there are one or two who might. There are several planes laid up which don't need much work on them to make them airworthy. I know several men who might consider a one way flight for a price."

"I'm interested."

"You're in a hurry, no doubt?"

"Yes—a great hurry."

"I thought so. I will be going over there this afternoon, so I will ask around. I'll see you at dinner time here. Of course, it will be very expensive as it is very risky. But a plane would be pretty cheap, I expect, as several owners have left. How many passengers would there be?"

"Two adults and two small children."

"I see. As I said, it is risky, especially with the anti-aircraft guns on the golf course. Also, on entering Thai airspace, there is the possibility of being shot down."

"I realize that, but it is their only hope," said Jake.

"I understand." The Frenchman finished his coffee, and getting up, shook hands all round. "A ce soir."

"Well," said Meg. "There is hope."

"Will you have enough money, Dad?"

"I hope so, Harry. Funds are becoming a bit low with all this travel."

"Do you think the old aunt will go too?"

"She will have no choice, if we manage to get them away."

22

Doctor Lian

A plane ride had been arranged. Tomorrow the pilot would see whether the plane was airworthy. He was prepared to take the risk accompanied by his wife and three small children. So they would be four adults and five children—the youngest a two-month old baby. If the plane was in a condition to fly, they would leave at dawn the next day.

The biggest problem was to get a message to Mr Lee. Everyone had an idea, and some were really far fetched. Both Anna and Harry wanted to go in disguise. But even if they could hide their blondness, their foreign accents would be a dead give-away. It was finally decided that Lian would pretend to be a medical assistant making a house call on the very elderly aunt.

So early in the afternoon, at the hottest time of day when people sleep, Jake and Lian drove to the Embassy, exchanged cars, and continued on, past the airport, to the old wooden house on the river bank. Jake ducked into a small store in sight of the old house, while Lian went on alone.

She was dressed smartly in a dark skirt and a white blouse. She strode purposefully towards the gate and guards, clutch-

ing a dark bag which held a thermometer, aspirins, one or
two small medicine bottles and a syringe.

She nodded to the guards, explaining that she had come
from the hospital to see the lady of the house. The guards did
not move, as they had been given no instructions. Lian patiently told them that she came regularly. They must allow
her in, as she was very busy and had other visits to make.
The guards shrugged, it sounded legitimate enough. While
one stayed at the gate, the other signalled Lian to follow him
into the house. So far so good.

François Lee was sitting in a chair by the window, gazing
across the river to Thailand. As they were under house arrest,
he was surprised to receive a visitor.

"The nurse for the lady," said the guard, gruffly. Lian
bowed slightly to Mr Lee.

"Just my regular visit," she explained, wondering what
his reaction would be, as they had never met.

"My sister is asleep."

"It will only take a short time, please take me to her."

Lian was nervous, especially as François Lee seemed re-
luctant to move, however, he gave a nod and lead the way
down the corridor. The guard followed, but at the door, Lian
told him to remain outside. He stopped in surprise, but
stayed behind the closed door without protest.

The room was large and dark. The old lady lay sleeping
quietly under a white mosquito net.

"Well?" François turned to look curiously at Lian.

As Lian slowly opened the bag and took out the contents
one by one, she quietly introduced herself and explained that
she came on behalf of Jake Porter. The man's eyes lit up with

relief—he'd believed Jake would come through but, even so, there had always been a slight doubt in the back of his mind that it might be impossible.

While his sister Aimée slept on undisturbed, François listened carefully to Jake's plan. He nodded slowly in agreement, "but there's a guard outside my room all night," he whispered.

"That's your problem," said Lian, "Mr Porter has his own. You must be ready. It will be very dangerous, but there will not be another chance."

"We'll be ready."

23

Trapped

The whole family were edgy as they waited to put the plans for the "great escape," as Harry had named it, into action. They put their equipment, consisting of fireworks and crackers, a metal cookie tray and a styrofoam box, together early in the morning, and then there was nothing else to do but wait until the late afternoon. Finally, there were just two hours more until curfew, and it was time to start.

Jake and Harry loaded the equipment into the car trunk, and Jake and Meg drove off, past the guards at the gate. This had been quite an issue, should Meg skulk under a blanket on the floor or not. In the end, she decided she should not, but then wondered whether she would regret that decision.

At the British Embassy, they transferred everything to Frank's car. Meg, driving the second car, followed Jake as far as the turnoff to their house, then continued on to the adjacent lane and parked in a field behind their house.

Harry was stationed beside the gates, which he opened as soon as he heard the family car approaching, so that Jake could drive in without slowing down and the guards would not realize that Meg was not in the car. Jake parked around the back of the house, out of sight.

Anna and Harry finally got started with their part of the plan. With their father, they climbed over the back wall to join their mother. (Lian was going to turn the lights on and off during the evening, so the guards would believe that the family were at home.)

They drove down to a house in a small riverside community, where Jake had arranged to rent an old, but well-oiled samlow for the night. They loaded everything into it, and then Jake slowly pedalled his family along the river bank into the gathering gloom.

They halted some distance away from Aunt Aimée's house, in the cover of some large bushes beside the river, and hid the samlow. Part of the plan was to cause a diversion with a small styrofoam raft on the river. This would be the launching pad for fireworks and crackers.

Harry dug a hole in the ground which he would use later to kindle a fire. A white-hot charcoal from the fire would then be put on a cookie tray on the raft and fireworks would be dropped on top. The whole thing would be pushed out into the current where, within seconds, it would be level with Aunt Aimée's house and the fireworks would explode.

He finished the preparations just as night fell. Then all they could do was to wait. The only relief was a small meal of hot soup from a Thermos flask and some sandwiches and chocolate biscuits. Time passed very slowly. Apart from insect noises and a couple of passing patrols, the quietness was complete.

At three-thirty, Jake stood up and stretched his cramped limbs, then with Harry's help, he pulled out the samlow and silently pedalled away, disappearing into the darkness.

Harry poured some paraffin onto the charcoal and lit the small fire, covering it with the cookie tray so no light would be visible. The charcoal was soon white hot. Very cautiously, Meg transferred the hot embers to the tray and placed it on the raft, while Harry held it steady in the water. Anna carefully dropped the fireworks on top and Harry waded out into the river and pushed the raft into the current. Glowing red, it bobbed and twirled downstream, and then erupted. Rockets leapt into the sky shooting red, silver and blue stars into the night, which exploded with a hideous noise, and Chinese firecrackers zigzagged erratically in all directions, shrieking loudly, before they plunged into the water where they sizzled and died.

Jake, already at the back door of the house, was delighted at the diversion, especially as the guards, and a passing patrol, rushed down to the water's edge shouting and firing at the raft. The raft valiantly bounced up from the water when hit and continued to glow red as it swept past them.

Jake knocked on the door, which opened immediately, and François pushed Guy and Pierre out to him. He followed, firmly holding his sister by the arm, and they all squeezed into the samlow.

The soldiers were still running along the river bank, shooting at the unsinkable raft. The charcoal continued to glow, although the fireworks display was over.

Jake found peddling up the steep path hard going in the dark, and his uncomplaining passengers were shaken and jolted to the bone. However, they soon reached the deserted road where Jake made a five-minute dash to the airport fence. In the shadow of a tree, the pilot was waiting for them beside the hole he'd cut. They all squeezed through and followed him out into the seemingly limitless blackness of the airfield. The small plane sat ready on the tarmac and the pilot's family squatted beneath the wing. The baby slept soundly. Jake helped them all to board. He whispered a final reminder to François to phone Louis from Udon, as well as counselling "You should all leave for France on the first flight out—I will not be able to rescue you again."

"I know. We can't thank you enough. Goodbye, I hope we will meet again one day."

"Yes," agreed Jake.

"Although I will never return to Laos as I'm old and change takes time, my grandsons and their children will return to cherish our beloved land."

"Let us hope so. Goodbye."

The engine caught, the small door banged shut and the plane swung onto the runway. To Jake, standing alone on the tarmac, the engine sounded very loud in the surrounding silence. Dawn was already breaking on the horizon. The plane rapidly lifted off, and immediately traces of fire flashed upward from the neighbouring golf course but the plane banked steeply as it turned towards the river. The fire from the ground was continuous, but the plane flew on valiantly, ducking and twisting until, with a cheeky waggle of its wings, it flew out of range.

Jake breathed a sigh of relief and ran back to the hole in the fence. There could be lots of trouble now. He pulled the samlow onto the road and just reached the cover of the dark lane before two jeeps raced into sight.

Jake did not pause, he pedalled furiously down the lane, praying he would meet no patrols. Meg and the children were anxiously waiting and leapt onto the moving samlow as he drew abreast. Jake pressed on without checking his speed, his breath rasping, his legs straining to reach the safety of the samlow owner's yard.

It was already daylight when they arrived. The man was washing himself beside a rain barrel of water. His wife was coaxing a small fire, and leaning patiently against their car, waiting for them, was Michel Lee.

24

Anna and the Marines

Jake abruptly stopped pedalling. Meg sat white-faced, clutching tightly the arm of the seat. Anna and Harry held their breath, curiously wondering what their parents would do now. The samlow man stood watching, while his wife ignored them all, intent on fanning the fire.

Michel Lee stepped forward with a tight smile on his face. "Well, the Scarlet Pimpernel returns," he said, and bowed mockingly.

"I don't believe we've met," said Jake flatly, dismounting from the hard seat and putting out a hand to help Meg down.

"No, that's true. Although I have had the honour of making the acquaintance of your wife and family. I'm Comrade Michel Lee, Chief of Police and Internal Security. You have caused me much personal trouble and, now, in my official capacity as well. I am arresting you and your family for assisting in the escape of traitors, who, if they are caught, will be shot."

Jake put his hands in his pockets and leaned wearily against the side of the samlow. He was exhausted after his unaccustomed recent exertions, but he felt a warm glow of satisfaction at his family's accomplishment. He just hoped that François Lee would make all possible haste to get his family over to France.

"I'm afraid that I don't know what you're talking about," he said. Michel hissed in annoyance and replied equally calmly, "I suppose you and your family were out for an early morning ride to admire the sunrise over the Mekong?"

"Yes."

Michel snapped his fingers in anger and shouted a command, and a dozen Pathet Lao appeared from behind the house and grabbed the Porters.

"Is this quite necessary?" demanded Jake. "There is no need to manhandle my family."

Michel Lee took no notice and, turning his back on them, strode away. The Pathet Lao followed with their prisoners.

Jake muttered angrily; Meg was trying to be aloof and dignified, even though she felt a mess after spending a night crouching in bushes; Anna glared at the young guards and thought how humiliating it all was. Thankfully all her friends had left so there was absolutely no chance that anyone would see her. Harry struggled and kicked at the shins of his captors, and wished Beauty were there to bite them hard on their backsides.

Several jeeps and drivers were parked behind the house. Michel climbed into the first. Jake and Harry were pushed into the back of the second by their guards, and Meg and Anna into the third. With a squeal of tires the jeeps pulled away, leaving the samlow driver, his wife, and a group of curious neighbours gaping after them.

"Well, what now, mother?"

"I don't know, Anna. This is a new experience for me, but we are in trouble all right. I hope Lian will go to Masters."

"But how soon?"

"Not until this afternoon. I wonder what they'll do with us? It's best we just keep quiet and let your father do the talking."

Anna nodded absently. The jeeps were now reaching the centre of town and were forced to slow down. The two soldiers, sitting on either side of her on the narrow bench, were uncomfortably aware of passersby staring at them. As they drew near the market, they could only creep along as the road was thronged with people loaded with baskets, push-carts laden with produce, small trucks with water melons and sugar cane, and bicycles and samlows. Anna bit her lip in concentration, waiting for the right moment. She was determined to escape, and where better than the crowded market. The jeeps were halted in a seething mass of people. She peered ahead, the road was completely blocked and they were right beside a gap in the market fence. Now or never.

The two guards were taken by surprise. They had been looking ahead, when suddenly Anna scrambled over the side and disappeared into the throng. It was impossible to see her, as she was dressed in black, the same as most of the people around her, with a black scarf over her blond hair. They jumped up and gazed out into the market place, but it was impossible to identify her amongst the crowd.

Three of the four guards jumped down, one remaining with Meg, his machine gun pointed at her stomach. Two raced through the gap in the fence and were soon lost from sight. The third pushed his way forward to Michel Lee, who shouted angrily at him and sent him off to search with the others.

Jake and Harry, both firmly held by their guards, looked back in surprise.

"Anna escaped!" shouted Meg. Her guard prodded her painfully in the ribs with his gun and told her to be quiet. Harry scowled in disbelief. He wished he could get away and angrily kicked out at his guards, but they just gripped him more tightly. Jake was anxious, where would Anna go? Would she be able to reach the British Embassy without getting caught? Now at least there was some hope of their being rescued. What a mess they were in.

Michel Lee stood up in the back of his jeep and shouted orders to the remaining soldiers. Meg's guard pulled her up and she was transferred to the second jeep. The first two jeeps moved off slowly, the third jeep stood waiting.

In ten minutes, they drew up at the entrance to the former American compound outside the city at KM-6. The gates swung open

immediately, and the jeeps swept up the road past the already neglected-looking bungalows, their overgrown gardens a riot of colour, and pulled up in front of the American school.

"I'm back at school," cried Harry. "I hope they let me empty my locker now I'm here."

They were hurried into a classroom, which had remained untouched since the students last left, believing they'd be back the next day. It was dusty, flowers had dried and disintegrated and goldfish lay dead in their aquarium. To Harry's disappointment, they were not taken into his classroom. Two armed guards stayed with them.

"Well," said Meg, sitting down at a desk, "now what's going to happen, I wonder."

"We may meet Souphanouvong himself, if we're lucky— this is the new government's HQ," commented Jake, mooching around the room, peering into desks and gazing at posters, artwork and notices on the walls.

"I hope Anna is alright," said Harry. "What a thing to do, lucky sod."

"Harry," said his mother sharply. "I hope she reached the Embassy," she sighed, with a worried frown on her face.

"I expect she will," said Jake. "She knows her way around, and luckily was dressed in those dark clothes."

"Lian will be worried. Really this is a nuisance, we'll probably be deported."

"I expect so," muttered Jake darkly. "Masters will be furious. It'll be highly embarrassing for the Brits."

"I'm so thirsty," sighed Meg. "What I'd do for a large cup of coffee."

*

Anna had darted away through the narrow alleys between the vegetable stalls. Several of the Lao she knew looked at her first in surprise and then alarm, as they realized she was being chased by the Pathet Lao.

Some of the young porters stood in the path of the soldiers and jostled and tripped them to allow Anna a few extra seconds. The soldiers swore and lashed out at the boys with their weapons, but the boys just laughed cheekily.

Once in the dark interior of the market building, Anna paused a moment wondering where to go. To hide or to continue? Her pursuers were not far behind. She was afraid to try to hide, in case one of the stall holders was unfriendly and gave her away, although she was sure that the majority would not. After a few minutes, she found herself on the far side of the market, almost out in the open air again, amongst the chicken and fish stalls where there was no cover. She kept on running, glancing quickly over her shoulder. She stumbled on the rough, uneven floor and fell against a large person.

"Anna, what's the hurry?" a laughing voice asked. Anna gasped in relief.

"Link, help me. I'm being chased by the PLs."

"Gee whiz, Anna. Come on quick, I have the pickup outside." The tall American marine grabbed Anna's hand, and they raced down the long, dark passageway between mountains of baskets and wickerware—sending rats scurrying to safety.

Without a pause, they leapt into the van parked at the curb. Link gunned the engine and they were away, just as the guards emerged from the market.

"Well, what have you been up to, young Anna?" demanded Link.

"Don't be so patronizing, Link. It's all far too complicated to explain now. However, my whole family were arrested, but I managed to escape into the market and those awful, flat-footed PLs were trying to recapture me."

"They still have your family?"

"Yes, I don't know where they are taking them, but I must

go to the British Embassy, Link. Would you drive me there?"

"Sure."

"Anyway, many thanks for saving me. It was really lucky that I ran into you as I wasn't sure where to go. I hope you won't get into trouble."

"Sure was. Don't worry about me, I'm not in uniform and we have more friends than enemies around here. I doubt whether anyone would give us away. Here's the Embassy. But I can't drop you there, duck down." And Link kept on driving past, as Anna doubled up on the wide front seat. Several jeeps were parked on the opposite side of the road watching. "Guess the place is staked out, now what?"

"I don't know. I can't go home as we have guards there as well."

"You'd better come back to the marine house, and we can try to phone the embassy to let them know what's happened."

"Great, as long as I don't get you into trouble. It'd be awful to be the cause of a diplomatic incident."

"Forget it kid, the guys will be delighted to have female company for breakfast."

It was true, Anna was given a warm welcome by the group of young marines and, within minutes, she was enjoying waffles with maple syrup and coffee.

The others were impressed that Link, the youngest and greenest marine, had rescued Anna from the clutches of the Pathet Lao. Now he was concerned about phoning the Embassy, "Hell, I don't know what I'm going to say to this guy—the phones are bound to be tapped. I'll give it a go, and if this Masters doesn't understand, Top, you'll have to go on an official visit."

"Hey, why me?" demanded the red-headed, strong-jawed marine sergeant.

"'Cause you're the senior guy and, with your charm, you'll be able to get past the receptionist."

"Okay, try and phone first."

"Good morning, Mr Masters's secretary speaking, can I help you?"

"Good day Ma'am, I sure hope so. It's kind of urgent that I speak to Mr Masters."

"He's in a meeting at the moment."

"Listen, Ma'am, it is important. Just call him out of the meeting."

"I couldn't do that."

"You must. It's a life-and-death thing, Ma'am."

"Just a minute then, please."

Link turned to the others, "The guy's in a meeting, of course, but I hope I persuaded that secretary to fetch him out."

A voice rumbled on the other end of the line.

"Good day, Sir, I'm calling on behalf of a friend of yours, Sir. He's in kinda trouble, said you were expecting it and needs your help."

"Can't you be more explicit, young man?"

"No Sir, I'm sure we are not the only ones listening. We tried to come to you but there is a stakeout, Sir."

"Yes, I know." said Masters, crossly. "We have lodged a complaint. Anyway, there is no need to be so mysterious, I know precisely who you mean. When did it happen? Just our mutual friend, I hope?"

"Gee, no, Sir. The whole family except Anna, she escaped, Sir."

"Good God, this is too much. Where is the child?"

"She's here, Sir."

"Good, keep her there. I'll set the ball rolling. When did you say it happened?"

"I didn't, Sir, but it was at dawn."

"At dawn, heh? Thank you for calling. Goodbye."

"Goodbye, Sir."

Link put down the phone and relayed the gist of the conversation to the others.

*

A long-faced Masters returned to his meeting. The ambassador looked at him enquiringly, "Well?"

"It was one of those young marines. The whole Porter family was arrested at dawn but the girl has managed to evade them and is now at the marine house."

"That's all we need. Four, or rather three, more of the Queen's subjects arrested, and one on the run. It seems to have become the fashion. Well, this meeting is adjourned. Go through the normal channels, Masters. Make an appointment for me after luncheon, and I will make another strong protest."

"There is one problem. They may have well deserved to be arrested," said Masters, diffidently.

"What did you say?" thundered the ambassador. "What has Jake Porter been up to?"

Masters nervously broke his pencil in half and cleared his throat. "He became rather involved, Sir," he said.

"Involved, involved in what?"

"Jake came a few days ago to warn me that he might be arrested and, if he was, asked to be rescued. He did rescue Bartlett and the Frenchman, you see Sir."

"I don't see, at all. What has he been doing?"

"Helping a family to escape."

"Why on earth did he have to meddle, were they friends?"

"No. In fact it was official, his children brought some passports back from Bangkok, but it became very complicated as the family are related to Michel Lee."

"That man? It really is too bad. The Canadian government should not involve its citizens in such matters when they are in our care. I suppose we'll have to try and free them. I expect they'll be deported—there will be no one left by Christmas at this rate. Set things in motion then, Masters."

25

At Souphanouvong's Pleasure

Anna was really worried about her family—but there was nothing much she could do. She knew she was being naive, but she hoped Masters, or possibly even the Ambassador himself, were planning a rescue. After all, that was what the Embassy was there for surely?

She was having a great time where she was. She'd never been looked after so well. She felt rather guilty because of her family and everything—and not only was Lincoln sitting beside her, trying to reassure her, but there were also another half dozen marines crowding around her. Wow! If only her school friends could see her now! Of course, when she would finally have time to write and tell them, they'd never believe her. It was just too amazing. Of course, she'd always had lots of friends, but her boyfriends had been her own age, while these marines were "older" men in their twenties. They were all amazingly handsome in their T-shirts and jeans—and dreamy when in uniform—and so polite. They were all giving her one hundred percent attention. Wow, it was great. Of course, she had to be honest, they were all probably really bored. Their lives were pretty dull as they had to keep a really low profile when not on guard duty at the embassy. And there was absolutely no competition. However, she was pretty and intelligent, even if she said so herself, and she had definite ideas of her own. She also knew not to flirt or be silly, just be herself. After all they were all in the middle of a scary adventure and perhaps they could do something for her family, instead of waiting for those stuffed shirts at the embassy.

*

At Souphanouvong's HQ at the former American compound, it was lunchtime. The changing of the guard also brought the prisoners bowls of vegetable soup and rice with fishpaste. It was amazing how instantaneously restorative food was. They all felt better physically and their spirits rose, although Meg still longed for coffee. Jake started pacing, wondering aloud why it was taking so long to release them.

"Do you think Anna's contacted the embassy, Dad?" asked Harry. He'd wolfed down his food and returned to the book he'd been reading, but he found Jake's pacing disruptive and decided to give it a rest.

"Yes, she must have by now. It's just going through the proper channels that takes so terribly long."

"At least Guy and Pierre must be reunited with their parents. Thankfully, we managed to get them all out. I do hope we're allowed to stay after this," said Meg.

"I doubt it," said Jake, gloomily.

"But we'd be an asset, keeping people from starving—we could provide food for several families."

"Life is cheap, Meg. They'd far rather get rid of us and let a few families starve—there are plenty of others."

"The teeming masses, Dad?"

"Yes, Harry, the teeming masses."

"Surely, they all have the right to live?"

"Of course. Everyone has the right to live and make the best of their lives, that is what we call freedom. But remember, freedom does not exist in the communist world. The people are directed and follow the party line. Those who think for themselves, or step out of line, are hooligans or dissidents. Now everyone is being brought into the system to work for the party for the good of the country and, as a reward, they will receive monthly handouts of basic essentials such as rice, milk for babies, sugar, soap and possibly some meat or fish. Those who don't fall into the correct categories will suffer and probably starve. Under the communist doctrine they are expendable anyway, either because they are too old, weak or handicapped, or because they are hooligans or dissidents. That is why we are afraid of communism, and why we fight it with all our might.

"Freedom is the most precious gift we can give our children and it is worth preserving. Life is no paradise, often the opposite, but within the framework of our society, one is free to choose one's path and to work for it. Of course, many are blessed with many more worldly goods than others, but in the communist world too, many are more equal than others. Many in the free world live in fear, loneliness or poverty, but it is worse in the communist world where many are imprisoned or banished for their beliefs; live drab lives, cramped lives; queue for endless hours for a bit of food for their families; are unable to practise their religion and are afraid to speak their minds—especially in front of their children. In fact, they are brainwashed by fear to live quiet ordinary lives. So Harry we must fight. We must help those who wish to escape, even if we find ourselves in uncomfortable situations like now. It is worth it, isn't it?"

"Of course, Dad."

So the day passed slowly. The young guards sat looking blankly ahead of them. Meg and Harry read, while Jake continued to pace, only occasionally stopping to sit on the edge of a desk and scowl at the two silent guards.

No one came near them and the afternoon seemed long. In frustration, Jake pounded his fist on a desk, knocking over a chair, and cried out, "Is nothing going to happen?" The guards jumped up in alarm, only to sit down again warily, as Jake continued to pace.

*

Meanwhile at the British Embassy, the Ambassador leant back in his chair, his elbows on the padded arms, his fingers poised as in prayer before his worried face. On the other side of the desk sat Masters and John from the Canadian embassy in Bangkok.

"I can't believe you people have brought about this terrible situation, John. The Porters are being held at Souphanouvong's pleasure, and there is nothing we can do except daily to keep on demanding their release. This could continue for months, for years."

"I can assure you, Sir, we never imagined anything like

this would happen. All they had to do was to carry in the passports. Of course, nothing went as planned right from the start, we never imagined Lee would care whether his brother and family remained in the country or not. We'd thought he'd be far too busy putting down the Mao loyalists and organizing the complete submission of the whole country."

"One should never take anything for granted. All this is most awkward. We have a fifteen-year-old girl sheltering in the marine house, while her family are being held at the new government HQ—I suppose we should be relieved that they're not in prison."

"All most irregular, Ambassador," fretted Masters. "I warned Jake, but he was determined to see the whole thing through. Why, oh why, did he have to involve the whole family?"

"But that was why this was such a great plan, the whole family were involved right from the start, as they were such a good cover," broke in John.

"Your government will have a lot to answer for, should anything happen to them—using women and children, whatever next?"

"They were an ideal cover."

"I know, I know, say no more. In any case most of the controlling force seemed to be aged about twelve."

"I'm worried about Anna being at the marine house, Sir. Is there no way we can remove her to a more suitable place?"

"Such as?"

"Well, your residence, Sir, with your wife."

"Hah, one moment you are using women and children as

good cover, and the next your Canadian-Scottish morals are outraged. I don't think it would be suitable to have a fugitive as a guest in my house. I'm sure the marines will be looking after her in an honourable manner, and after all she is merely a child."

"Hardly a child, sir, and in any case, is it quite right that we should expect the Americans to harbour a fugitive for us?"

"Well, they rescued her," said a petulant Masters.

"You mean she should have been left to be recaptured?"

"No, of course not. But can we just leave things as they are for twenty-four hours, instead of trying to create further complications?

"Yes, Sir, I take the hint. But I think I'll just go and check up on her, so may I have a car and driver?"

"I suppose so, if you insist."

John stood up. "Thank you, Sir." He quickly left the room, before the ambassador should change his mind, shutting the door loudly behind him.

"He's annoyed with us, Masters," said the Ambassador.

"Yes, Sir, but I don't know what he expects us to do."

"Quite."

26

Waiting

John was warmly welcomed by Anna and the marines, who drew him into their circle around a low coffee table.

"When did you arrive in Vientiane, John?" asked Anna.

"This morning. I imagined it would be a routine visit but it's hardly that. It's hard to believe what's happened to you all."

"Well it did become a bit involved. I'm fine, but I'm really worried about my parents and Harry. Will they be released soon?"

"I honestly don't know. They're being held at Souphanouvong's pleasure."

"Gee, that sound's pretty bad, Sir," chipped in Lincoln, bringing John an ice-cold beer.

"Can't you do something, John. After all we managed to spirit Mr Lee and his family out, in fact some of them twice, and Dad found and helped release Mr Bartlett and the French guy. Can't you do the same?"

"I think we should wait awhile, Anna. There is no point in being hasty and regretting it. You don't want to be deported."

Anna sighed. Link gave her a sympathetic smile, while the other marines looked thoughtful. John watched them uneasily.

"Please no one do anything foolish," he appealed.

"No, of course not, Sir," said Top firmly. "However, what is the British Embassy doing?"

"Well, nothing really. They'll make an official request every day for their release."

Glances passed between the marines, and Anna jumped up and said, "John, I really think I should go home. Lian and the others will be worried sick, and I should be there with them."

"Anna, on no account must you leave here. You're liable to be arrested the minute you leave the compound. I'll go and see how things are at the house."

Anna sighed as she watched John drive away in the embassy car. She wished she'd been able to leave with him. She was as much a prisoner as the rest of her family.

"Come on, cheer up," said Link, giving her a friendly hug. "It will only be a day or two, and then you'll probably be able to return home."

Rollo, a tall chunky blond, observed in his slow drawl to the room at large, "I guess we should come up with a plan, guys, no good just sitting waiting for those embassy people to send more notes. How about some action?"

The others clustered around eagerly. "Well, Top," queried Little John, a large freckled six-footer. Top flexed his muscles thoughtfully, and gazed around at his men and the pretty girl in their midst. It was crazy, against policy, but ... "Sure why not? Sleep on it and we'll pool ideas in the a.m."

*

It was late afternoon when John arrived at the Porters' house. The guards were still at the gate, and Beauty came running down the drive, barking joyfully, as he climbed out of the car. Alerted by the dog, the rest of the household came running out to meet him and he was swept into the house.

"Please, tell us the news," demanded Lian, as they clustered around. John looked gravely at the anxious faces.

"It is not good news. Mr and Mrs Porter and Harry are still being held. We've not been able to see them. Anna, however, is with friends and is fine—although not able to return here. She's very anxious about you all."

"We are so afraid. What will happen to them?"

"I don't know. We just have to wait and see."

27

Skyfighters

Vang, Lian's husband, had been dragged out of bed in front of his terrified elderly parents and three small daughters the night after the communist takeover. A stolid, loyal man, he'd been a trusted employee in a government office and had been one of the first to be denounced and arrested for re-education, along with the minister, the under-minister and various other long-standing civil servants.

He had been pushed into the back of a covered truck, which had been parked outside his house, with its engine running, in the early hours of the morning. When he picked himself up and looked around, he found himself among many other frightened, bewildered and angry men. Most were only partially clothed, not having been given time to dress, and they were shivering in the cold night air.

The truck had driven through the night and for two more days. It stopped only to refuel, or to air and feed the prisoners in secluded spots. Food had been provided by terrified villagers along the way. The men were exhausted, as they had to stand most of the time because of lack of space, bumping and jolting over rough, unmade roads. Those of the men who were elderly and frail were given places so they could lean against the sides of the truck.

Finally, on arriving at their destination, they found themselves in virgin forest where they were immediately issued with axes and machetes to clear a space and fell trees for their living quarters. Around them other groups were doing the same.

Fortunately Vang, although used to office work, was strong and used to cultivating his own small patch of land. But the frail and elderly in his group were berated by the young guards, as they attempted to swing the heavy axes and clear the harsh undergrowth with their bare hands. Dirty, bruised and bleeding, they lay where they were when darkness came, too exhausted to seek any shelter.

Time passed monotonously with hard work, inadequate food, long evenings of political education, and lonely, fearful nights spent on the hard ground in the rude barracks they had built. Mosquitoes showed no mercy in the dark.

Many of the older men became sick, and some of them died due to lack of medicines. There was no communication with the outside world apart from news brought by new arrivals. The few men who managed to escape, carried one or two verbal messages for their companions back to their anxious families.

Vang spent most of his time with two other men. One was an old boyhood friend, Nao, and the second was a Mao, called Lam, who had been caught while sheltering for the night in the village. They were all determined to escape, and make their way to Lam's village, high in the mountains, where they would join the skyfighters.

The skyfighters were young Mao men who had vowed to continue the fight against the communists and not cut their hair until they succeeded in overthrowing them.

One night, under the cover of darkness, the three men slipped away, with a handful of rice in their pockets and whispered messages from the others to carry back with them to Vientiane—if they made it back.

The journey took a long time. The going was rough through thick undergrowth and mud, and across swollen rivers. They always stayed alert for patrols and other travellers. Leeches, flies and mosquitos attacked them. At night the sure-footed Lam crept into villages to steal corn, or anything else edible, from the storehouses on stilts. Whatever it was, they gnawed it raw, together with roots, leaves and insects collected on their way.

Lam led them with assurance towards his village in the jungle-covered mountains, and they thankfully reached it one moonless night. Leaving Vang and Nao some distance away, Lam crept nearer to signal the guard, who kept a constant watch day and night for communist patrols. They were led triumphantly into the village where everyone came out to greet them. Lam's mother and wife immediately started to prepare a meal, while they washed and changed into clean clothes and covered their many cuts, scratches and bites with herbal salves.

The people sat around a small, flickering fire in the centre of the village. The wooden houses, built on stilts, blended into the black backdrop of the protective forest. The three men were given bowls of rice, pork and vegetables and fiery rice whisky to drink.

Vang was exhausted, and once he felt comfortably full, and lightheaded from the whisky, he was unable to keep his eyes open. He was barely able to concentrate on what was being said. Sometime later, a gentle hand on his shoulder woke him. As in a dream, he was only vaguely aware of the red embers of the fire, the embroidered clothes of the women, and the circle of pale faces in the darkness, before he was led away to sleep.

By noon the next day, they felt refreshed and had breakfasted on rice and vegetables washed down with tiny cups of local tea. They sat in a circle, on the hard-packed earth beneath a house, with a group of skyfighters. The men were lean and tough, dressed in black clothes, similar to their own, and their long hair was tied back from their faces with black bands.

The leader, a grim-faced man in his thirties, told the newcomers about the recent raids they had made, resulting in the stealing of weapons, the destruction of police stations and arsenals, and the killing of patrols. There had been a few casualties but no deaths. As well as Lam, two other Mao men had been picked up, and although they had heard nothing from them, they believed they would eventually return too.

They were now planning their biggest raid, in coordination with other groups, to storm and burn Souphanouvong's HQ and to take hostages—Souphanouvong and Lee. Scouts had been watching the camp, noting the different buildings, planning where the fence should be breached and their routes of escape. Plans were brought out to be studied, and each man went over his special duties and the newcomers were given their orders.

As dusk approached, the papers were rolled away. The married men went home to their families, while the younger men gathered near the pretty village girls.

Lam, Nao and Vang being married men, went to sit beneath Lam's house. His wife brought them drinks and they discussed what they had just heard. Lam's two small children soon came scampering down the steep steps to play and, as darkness fell, Lam's elderly father brought the family buffalo beneath the house for the night. The mild mannered pink beast was the family's wealth and greatly cherished.

The next day the skyfighters, accompanied by Nao and Vang, left the village on foot for Vientiane. A mist hovered over the valley as they rapidly descended the worn track through the jungle. The men had an assortment of weapons, some given them by the Americans, Russian ones stolen from the Pathet Lao, as well as machetes and hunting knives.

By nightfall they reached an unpaved road and, keeping to the shadows, hurried along until they reached a straggling village, silent in the pale moonlight. Some thin, mangy dogs barked and growled at them as they passed, but the villagers were too afraid to be curious. At the last house along the road, they turned up a small winding path through a banana grove, at the far side of which was an old wooden house. The verandah railing sagged with age, and the piles of wood neatly stacked beneath the house scented the air with the sweet smell of freshly sawn timber. The group of men stopped and squatted in the shadow of the trees, as the leader climbed swiftly up the outside stairs and disappeared into the house.

Five minutes later, he reappeared and beckoned to the others.

Silently they climbed up into the house. Inside, the room was dark apart from a single candle burning on a low table. The one roomed house was filled with black clad men crouching on the floor or leaning against the walls. Vang and Nao thankfully sank down near the door, tired but bursting with suppressed excitement.

The men sat in complete silence while the three leaders talked quietly around the paper strewn table in the flickering light. Finally, their meeting concluded, they rejoined their men, dividing them into twos and threes to make their way into Vientiane. By tomorrow night, they would all be in position around Souphanouvong's HQ, waiting for the moment to strike.

28

No Special Privileges

As dawn approached, Harry rolled over on the tiled floor. He groaned loudly and sat up. Every bone in his body ached, and he felt cold and stiff. He stood up and stretched. His parents were also awake and moaning in misery, rubbing their eyes and pushing back their hair from their faces.

"I feel terrible," sighed Meg.

"You look it too, Mum," said Harry mischievously.

"Harry," snapped his father, "apologize to your mother."

"Please Jake," said Meg wearily, "there's no need, he's speaking the truth—after one night in the bushes and another on the floor, I don't look my best. Do you realize, we've been here twenty-four hours?"

"I know," said Jake. "Today, I'm going to demand to see Souphanouvong or Lee. This is ridiculous."

Yesterday Harry had found it quite an adventure to be held prisoner by armed guards. Although he was still mad that his sister had been the one to have the idea to escape. If only he'd thought of it first! He could kick himself. But he was really getting bored now, and lying on the floor all night was pretty grim—although far worse for his aged parents.

He was really glad when the door opened at six, and the relief guards brought in bowls of tea and rice. When they had eaten, they were escorted, one by one, to the washroom to tidy themselves the best they could under the gaze of a guard.

Harry hadn't meant to be rude to his mother. She always put up with a lot, living in the difficult places their Dad's job took them. And he really didn't worry what *he* looked like. Who wanted to wash in any case? He could quite happily go without washing for days, although granted it wasn't too nice when his teeth became furry!

Once they had all had their wash, Jake asked the guards if he could see Michel Lee. They smiled nervously and said nothing, simply watched him warily.

The morning dragged on very slowly. At noon, the guards were changed and again Jake asked to see Michel Lee. The men muttered amongst themselves, smiled in embarrassment at Jake's angry red face, but remained silent.

"I'm afraid we'll just have to be patient, dear," said Meg with a sigh.

"I know, but I'm not a patient man," growled Jake, furiously pacing up and down.

"Well, eat your lunch, Dad."

"Ohh . . . " Jake moaned in exasperation. But he sat down and angrily shovelled in his lunch with his fingers. They'd not been provided with utensils.

At five, Jake was called to the door. Meg and Harry tried to follow but the guards barred their way.

Jake was escorted across the school's baseball diamond to a large bungalow. Michel Lee was waiting for him, seated stiffly behind a desk.

Jake stood silently at the door, the guard beside him.

"Come in Mr Porter," said Lee. "I believe you wished to see me?"

"Yes," replied Jake, moving into the room. There was no other chair so he was obliged to stand before the desk in front of Lee. "What's the meaning of holding us here? Are we to be charged with something? I demand to see my ambassador."

"You demand, Mr Porter?"

"Yes."

Michel Lee glared coldly at Jake for a long silent moment, then said in a clear, precise voice, "You have no rights, Mr Porter. You, your wife and son are being held at Comrade Souphanouvong's pleasure—indefinitely."

"Indefinitely?" gasped Jake. "But we're being held in a classroom without sleeping or washing facilities."

"Mr Porter we are a revolutionary government, our prisoners do not have special privileges. You're lucky not to be in prison, or to have been taken out and shot. But I will see that you are issued with some sleeping mats." And with a dry nod, Lee indicated that the interview was over.

29

Reconnaissance

As Anna stood under the shower, she was thinking about the evening before—it had been special and she relived it moment by moment. They had sat up late, watching a movie and then Link had put on some music and they'd danced. Little John and the sergeant had been playing pool at the far end of the rec. room, and the steward had been polishing glasses behind the bar. The other marines had disappeared upstairs.

Link had held her close, and she was glad of his comforting shoulder as she was tired—and she also felt depressed even though she was so happy. She had felt really mixed up, it was scary. Link had said, "You know Anna, it was my lucky day running into you in the market."

"Me too, Link. It would have been so humiliating to have been caught."

"Well, I guess we're both lucky." He'd held her so close, she could feel his heart beating. He'd lifted her chin and their lips met in a long, tingling kiss.

"You're my girl now," he'd said and twirled her around the room.

Out of the corner of her eye, she'd seen Little John nudge Top in the ribs with his cue, and he'd whispered loudly "I guess the babes are falling in love." The sergeant had chuckled, "They make a swell young couple."

Anna closed her eyes and, as the water cascaded down, she remembered the kiss and the sergeant's words in the background. She sighed happily. She felt grownup. She wouldn't tell Link she was only fifteen, probably he thought she was at least seventeen or even eighteen. She must remember to be dignified and not giggle.

She giggled at the idea and then leaped out of the shower as she heard the clatter of feet on the stairs as a gong announced breakfast. She didn't want to miss any possible ideas for rescuing her family.

As she slid into the empty chair beside Link, he gave her a possessive smile and squeezed her hand under the table. He looked very handsome dressed in his immaculate uniform, ready to go on duty at the embassy.

The other marines all nodded in a friendly manner, but were too busy eating to speak. Finally, the sergeant pushed back his empty plate and looking around the table enquired,

"Well, any ideas?"

Little John, with his mouth full, mumbled, "I guess the only way is to go right in."

"Someone will have to recce the layout," commented Brett.

"Okay, first things first," said Top. "Brett and Rollo, you're off duty, so change into something dark and go up to the HQ. Don't get caught or you'll be shot for spying. Find out where Souphanouvong and Lee are quartered, where the prisoners are being held, traffic, security, etcetera, etcetera.''

"How about lunch?" asked Rollo, anxiously.

"Take a packed lunch. We'll all meet back here at six.''

*

Brett and Rollo left their jeep in a small copse and waded
around the edge of a muddy paddyfield to the perimeter of
the former American compound. They stopped briefly to
wring out their wet trouser legs.

"We'd better make for that belt of trees," said Brett,
pointing to a large stand of trees at one end of the fenced-in
area.

"Do you think they'll have patrols outside the wire?"
queried Rollo.

"I doubt it, they're safer inside."

They went on carefully, until they reached the trees where
they could see a well worn path inside the fence.

"I guess we better separate and meet up for lunch."

"Okay. I'll swing round to watch the gate, and you can go
up to the houses. We can leave the lunch up a tree and meet
back here at twelve."

"Twelve-thirty, Rollo."

"Okay, twelve-thirty."

Rollo hoisted the green backpack with the food up
amongst the thick foliage of a tree and made sure it was
secure. Then, armed with notebooks and binoculars they
parted company, unaware that they were being watched by
two Mao hidden in the undergrowth a few yards away.

"What are two Americans doing here?"

"Same as us, no doubt."

"Shall I look in the bag?"

The younger man cautiously dislodged the bag with some difficulty, as he was quite a bit shorter than the marine, and brought it back to the other Mao. They looked inside.

"Felang food and Cokes."

"Hungry?"

"Of course."

"We'll just take half—there's enough for a dozen people here. These young Americans have large appetites." They laughed softly and, stuffing one lunch back into the bag, returned it to the tree.

"No wonder they all grow so big—but it tastes good."

They slowly demolished most of it, savouring every mouthful, and stuffed some bread and cookies into their pockets for later. The elder of the two sighed in satisfaction and said, "bury the can. I'm going to have a short sleep, wake me in half an hour, then I'll watch for you."

His companion nodded in agreement. He carefully buried the can and then sat silently, but fully alert, as his companion curled up and immediately fell asleep. It was pleasant to be waiting with a full stomach for a change.

Some three hours later, Brett returned to the tree and pulled down the bag. He retreated with it into the undergrowth, where he sat down on a log and opened it.

"Strange," he muttered, "only one lunch and one soft drink. Rollo must have sneaked back to eat, the greedy pig." He tucked into his food with gusto. He had eaten a good half when Rollo came staggering back, hot and exhausted, and threw himself down beside Brett.

"Gee, am I ever hot and hungry."

"You can't be hungry. When did you come back for your lunch?"

"What do you mean? Gi'me my lunch."

"But there was only one here, and I've almost finished it."

"You must be joking." Rollo sat up, and dragged the bag towards him.

"I'm not, honest. When I pulled the bag down, there was only one lunch and one can."

"Oh no, we've been robbed. I'll starve to death."

"Did you really not take it?"

"No, I was watching the gate and dodging patrols all morning. I can't believe it. You saw that there were two lunches—who can have taken them?"

"Here, take the rest of this. Hurry though, we're probably being watched, although they must be friendlies as they only took half and haven't killed us."

Rollo stuffed the last of the cookies hastily into his mouth, washing it down with the last few mouthfuls of Coke and threw the empty can into the bushes.

"Okay, let's circle round, I think they're over to the right."

"I agree, come on slowly now."

The two Mao watched the marines. "They're coming to look for us."

"Yes. Stay still, they'll probably walk right past."

"Don't be so sure."

Brett saw them first, signalled to Rollo, and together they pounced.

"Okay soldier, we come out. We no fight. Friends, heh?"

Rollo looked down at the young smiling Mao beneath him, "Did you take my food?" he demanded angrily.

"Yes, very sorry, but we have no food, and temptation was mighty strong. You have plenty."

Brett looked at the man he held, older, very thin but strong and wiry. He turned to Rollo. "Well, I guess they're not PLs," he said. "Do we let them go?"

"No, not yet. Say, where did you learn English?" Rollo asked the younger man under him.

"I work USAID for five years."

"What are you doing here?"

"If you get off, I tell you. You very heavy guy." Rollo chuckled and eased himself off. They all squatted comfortably together to talk.

"We're skyfighters," explained the young one. "We look around here, see you put your bag in tree and we ask what young marines do here. We look in bag. We are hungry, plenty of food—so we take half."

"Okay, fair enough, I guess."

The older man spoke rapidly to the younger in Lao, and the latter translated for the others.

"My friend ask what you do here?"

Rollo and Brett exchanged glances, "we're trying to locate some prisoners," said Brett.

"Prisoners? Here?"

"Yup."

"Who are they?"

"A Canadian family."

The Mao talked earnestly together, and then the young

one spoke slowly, "This is a big problem. We not know prisoners held here. You must talk to our leaders."

"Why, what's the problem?"

"You talk to leaders," repeated the Mao, giving nothing away.

"Guess they're planning a raid," muttered Rollo to Brett.

"Oh shit, if they blow the place apart, the Porters could go up with it. Do you suppose they're all around us?" Brett glanced around, but nothing moved in the heat of the afternoon.

"Where are your leaders?"

"You wait, please. They come soon."

"Okay," agreed Brett and Rollo, and the two Mao bowed and melted silently away into the trees.

"I guess, we just have to wait."

"Did you see where the Porters were being held?"

"Yes. I saw food being carried into the primary classrooms at noon, and two different PLs came out five minutes later. Presumably a change of guard. Several houses on the far side of the baseball field are heavily guarded, I should imagine they are the VIP quarters."

"Good work, Brett," said Rollo, impressed. "There was lots of traffic at the gate. A strong guard, and everyone checked and all vehicles searched thoroughly. Patrols around the perimeter seemed very frequent almost every ten minutes. Three men in a patrol. It's a fortress. Still, if we have help tonight, we could be successful."

The two marines settled back for a long wait. An hour passed slowly. There was the noise of traffic on the road; the sound of PL patrols within the fence, but the woods were quiet, apart from birds and insects among the trees.

At five, when the shadows had lengthened among the trees, and Brett and Rollo were beginning to be anxious and restless, the two Mao returned with their leaders.

They all bowed, eyeing each other suspiciously, before settling down into a tight circle, hidden by the undergrowth. Two of the leaders spoke some English, and they questioned the marines. Finally one said, "This makes a difference to our plan. We intend to raid and take hostages tonight, but now we learn there are prisoners. We will accompany you to your meeting." He turned and spoke rapidly to the others. An agreement was reached, and the two English-speakers stood up ready to go with Brett and Rollo.

30

Joining Forces

Anna sat waiting at the meeting table. She felt nervous and excited all at the same time. The marine sergeant sat at the head, and all the other marines were there, with the exception of those on duty at the embassy, and Brett and Rollo.

Where could Brett and Rollo be. She was worried for them. She was afraid they'd been caught and, if so, it would be her fault, for being impatient for her family's release. Not wanting to wait patiently like Masters and the Ambassador. "Please God, let them be alright!"

"They're late," growled Top, looking at the wall clock. It was six-fifteen.

"Do you think they've been caught, Sarge?" enquired a freckled marine, across the table.

"Heck, I sure hope not."

"I heard a jeep, Sarge," cried Little John, leaping up and striding to the window.

"Sit down, the meeting is brought to order."

The other marines glanced at each other but were silent. They knew Top well. He'd been worried as well, but now would be coldly furious when Rollo and Brett came in twenty minutes late.

The door of the dining room burst open, and Brett strode in followed by the two Mao leaders, with Rollo in the rear. The sergeant and marines jumped up in surprise.

"Sir, we apologize for being late. May we present Colonel Xuan Thong and Colonel Sanaphanya of the Skyfighters."

The sergeant stepped forward and saluted the two Mao who, smiling a little, returned the salute.

"Chairs," the sergeant snapped, and two marines vacated their chairs for the visitors.

"Sir, permission to speak. We met up with two Mao Sky-fighters, and we learned that they intend to blow up the HQ tonight and take hostages. They didn't know there were prisoners, but once we told them, they fetched their leaders."

"I see. It must have been crowded around the perimeter." He turned towards the visitors. "Are you planning to go in tonight?"

"Yes. We have three divisions, all homing in on the target at three a.m. We intend to destroy the complex and capture Souphanouvong and Lee. We're well armed, and we have been watching the place for many days. However, somehow we missed the arrival of your friends. We were not aware of prisoners."

"I see, Colonel. As far as we know, the Porters are the only prisoners. Can you confirm this, McIntyre?"

"Yes, Sir," said Brett. "We observed food being carried into the primary-school building. Food for three, Sir. Two guards are with them around the clock."

"Good. Well, if you intend to go in tonight, we'll have to rescue this young lady's family at the same time," said the sergeant briskly, nodding towards Anna. The Mao looked at her curiously and bowed.

At that moment, there was a hesitant knock on the door and the steward entered.

"Yes, Nguyen?" snapped the sergeant, annoyed at the interruption.

"Very sorry, Sir, but Mr John Lawrence-Smith would like to speak to you."

The sergeant swore in exasperation. "The Canadian Embassy man—excuse me a moment." He pushed back his chair, "I'll just go and speak to him outside."

"No need to move, Sergeant," said a voice from the door, and John walked in, smiling cheerfully. "Evening all," he continued, his eyes narrowing as he glanced at those gathered around the table.

"Evening, Sir." chorused the marines.

"Hello, John," said Anna, grinning widely.

"I can see you're plotting, Sergeant."

"Plotting, Sir?" laughed the sergeant. "Please, join us."

"Thanks." John took the vacant chair beside Little John and sat smiling, waiting for the sergeant to continue.

"Sir, may I first introduce Colonel Xuang Thong and Colonel Sanaphany. Mr John Lawrence-Smith from the Canadian Embassy in Bangkok." They all smiled and bowed politely.

"Well, as I was saying, it's a pretty kettle of fish," and he stopped abruptly.

John looked around the table at the grinning marines and the startled Mao. Anna bit her lip, determined not to giggle with Link sitting beside her. John was really being delightfully wicked. She was so glad to see him, and she knew he was joking because he felt awkward barging in on their meeting. But he was tough and wanted to be there. At least he'd put them all at their ease.

The sergeant took a deep breath and said firmly, "It would be far better for you not to stay, Sir. It would be just as well if you were not aware of our plans."

"For tonight?"

"Yes. We intend to rescue the Porters and they'll be taken across the river. Your job, Sir, will be to see to their belongings and further travel plans from Thailand."

"As you wish, Sergeant. You're probably right, better if I know nothing—so dull. I'll go and see to a reception committee tomorrow morning. Any idea where or when?"

The sergeant turned to the Mao, "Would some of your people be able to ship the four of them across?"

The two colonels talked quickly together. "We can arrange a boat just before dawn. But it will be up to you, Sergeant, to get them there."

"Wilco."

"Fine. What happens to Anna?"

"We'll look after her, Sir," said Link. "She'll cross over with the rest of her family." He looked at the sergeant for confirmation. The sergeant nodded in agreement.

Anna had sat silently, listening to this exchange. But there were so many lose ends, and she had to know.

"But, John, what about the animals, Lian and the others?"

"Don't worry, I'll look after everything, I promise."

"Oh dear." She felt so upset and helpless. It would be absolutely awful for Lian and the others. How could they possibly just abandon them? What about all their things, and the rabbits? But most of all, Lian, her daughters, and poor old Tee and Somphong—it was just not possible to leave without making any arrangements.

"You must trust me, Anna. You must leave as soon as the others are rescued."

"I know. It's just Lian and the others, we have to do something . . ." and she said no more, sat quietly looking at the table, blinking back sudden tears.

"Anna, I promise to look after them and see they're alright. Really, I will. I know how important they are to your family, and I would never dare face your father again if everything wasn't done properly. He'd be back in a flash—and we can't let that happen. Honestly, trust me."

*

Half an hour later, John was seated across the desk from the British Ambassador. A ruffled, disgruntled Ambassador, puffing angrily at his before-dinner cigar.

"You say the Porters will be in Thailand early tomorrow? How do you know? How is it possible?"

"Shall we just say, a little bird, Sir. It's far better that you don't know how, just as I have been told not to know."

"Who told you?" snapped the Ambassador.

"The people involved in transporting them across the Mekong."

"I suppose it's those Yanks. They are always ready to dash in, regardless of consequences. I think sometimes they imagine they're in one of their Western movies. Oh well, I suppose it's out of our hands. At least, Porter and his family will enjoy it."

31

The Raid

The marine house buzzed with nervous energy and suppressed excitement as the marines dressed in black clothing and blackened their faces. They were ready and impatient to move out.

Anna, dressed in her black peasant clothes with her fair hair covered with a black kerchief, sat nervously on the edge of a couch, hand in hand with Link. "I'm scared," she whispered.

Link smiled reassuringly and put his arm around her shoulders.

"It'll all work out, you'll see," he whispered. "They're a great bunch of guys and Top has lots of experience. With all the cover we're going to get from the Mao, it will be a cinch, and you'll be in Thailand before you realize it."

"I know," murmured Anna, looking around the room at the young men. That's just the point, she thought. Once I'm in Thailand, I'll not see you again. She was very taken with this serious, considerate marine. It was the first time she'd fallen for such a mature and handsome man. How was she going to bear leaving him behind? She mentally shook herself. Now was not the time for such thoughts, she had to concentrate on the present. It was scary and exciting to be part of a real raid to rescue her parents and Harry. This was what you read about in novels and heard about on the news. She was actually taking part in the real thing with US marines and Skyfighters. While the marines went in, she would stay in the truck. Wow!

*

The truck lurched and jolted along the small country lanes until they reached a deserted house about half a mile from their objective, where they parked. The marines clambered down. Link was out last, taking a moment to give Anna a hurried kiss. She clung to him briefly and then he was gone. They were all gone. They had silently disappeared into the black night, leaving her quite alone in the truck. Nothing moved. She could see no distance at all, as it was so dark. All she could sense was the strong smell of gas from the cooling truck engine; and the only sounds were her own breathing, and a small rasp of metal as she moved her feet on the floor.

She was terrified. She hated being alone. Every minute seemed an eternity. When would the raid begin? It was unbelievable that there were men all around in the impenetrable darkness. What if they were caught? What if they were walking into a trap? Why were they taking so long? Anna glanced at the illuminated hands of her watch. Only eight minutes had passed since the marines had left, and zero hour was on the half hour. Two more minutes.

*

Stealthily Brett and Rollo led the other marines to a point in the fence that was nearest to the school buildings. They walked quite a distance, at least the length of two city blocks. But they moved quickly, and once there, Little John cut the wire. They slipped through, diving for cover under a garden hedge before the patrol approached.

The patrol clumped along noisily, their weapons clanking against their belts and their boots snapping dry twigs in their path. As soon as they were out of earshot, the marines moved on to the school complex and, very cautiously, took up their positions around one of the doors, which lead to the primary classrooms.

There was not a sound. The night air was heavy with the scent of flowers. The moon was still hidden, so the only light came from the street lamps, which cast long pale shadows on the ground around the baseball diamond.

Suddenly, the silence was rent with loud explosions, the sound of gunfire, shouting, screaming and the sky was ablaze with light. Back in the truck, Anna sat shivering, praying over and over "Dear God, keep them safe."

The marines rushed the door: sending the two guards, standing behind it, flying. Jake, Meg and Harry scrambled up in surprise, and allowed themselves to be pushed out of the classroom by these black-faced "friendlies."

Outside, they were greeted by a nightmare—buildings, the surrounding trees, and small dancing figures all burning brightly. The gunfire was steady. Vehicles were exploding,

and more and more antlike figures were pouring out of the
buildings. They came out shooting but were being mowed
down instantly.

Urged on by the tense marines, the Porters stumbled along
behind the sergeant, keeping to the shadows. The night was
as bright as day. Although their guards had been dealt with,
a nearby patrol had spotted them and were firing at them,
and the marines were returning fire. The heavy scent of
flowers had been overcome by the stench of gunfire and
burning. Finally, gasping for breath and retching with the
smoke, they were through the hole in the fence and into the
undergrowth on the other side. They stopped for a minute,
while Top did a quick head count. Then on they plunged,
through the trees and tall grass.

*

From under the canvas cover of the truck, Anna peered out
onto the illuminated landscape. It was like the pictures she'd
seen of hell. Fires burning everywhere and the terrible
sounds of guns, the whoosh of flames, screams and shouts.
Then from behind, she heard the sound of trucks on the
road—help was coming to the beleaguered troops. The gunfire didn't slacken. Not only had the smell of burning
reached her, but also flying ash and burning particles were
raining down on the canvas roof and the ground around her.

Then, to her joy, she heard the sound of running feet from
the side of the house as well as shooting very close at hand.
They were coming: but someone must be following them.
Then a group of people appeared and she pulled open wide

the canvas back.

They were free. She stretched down to help her mother and brother aboard as they were shoved up from behind by the marines. They were all gasping and coughing from the smoke. Her father and the sergeant came bursting around the corner of a house and climbed into the front of the truck. The engine started smoothly. Other marines came running, firing steadily. Bullets landed around them, one ripping the canvas roof, as they crouched in the bottom of the truck. The truck moved forward without lights, two more marines leapt in and then others. Only Link was still out there, firing at the rapidly approaching PLs.

"Come on, Link."

"Link!" screamed Anna. Link turned and ran to catch the moving vehicle, just as the Pathet Lao appeared in the clearing. He leapt into the back, gave a low cry as he was hit, and fell sprawling into Anna's arms. The truck picked up speed and headed towards the river.

32

The Final Crossing

"Link," gasped Anna, "he's been hit." She looked around for help.

"Let me see," said a cool firm voice. It was Brett, and he knelt beside the unconscious Lincoln. "Light, please." A bright beam shone onto the bloodsoaked clothing of the young marine. Anna held him in her arms. Meg watched anxiously from behind, while Harry turned away his head, feeling sick at the sight of so much blood.

Brett expertly examined the wound. Little John opened a first-aid pack, and the wound was cleaned and bound tightly.

"That will do for now," muttered Brett. "He needs proper attention asap."

"Is it very bad?" whispered Anna.

Brett glanced up at her white face and said brusquely, "He's lost a lot of blood, but he'll live, never fear. No lousy red bullet is going to kill old Link."

They were driving along the main road still without lights, and the sergeant was pushing the truck to its limit. So far nothing seemed to be following them. If they could remain on the smooth surface of the highway, they would reach the boat in no time at all. The sooner they were able to drop off their passengers, the sooner they would be able to return to their base.

Turning a slight bend in the road, they were confronted by headlights coming towards them, and the sergeant deftly swerved the truck off the road. The truck ploughed its way through a ditch, over a low bank and into a small plantation of bamboo. Top cut the engine. Those in the back were bumped and tossed about. Anna, Rollo and Little John braced themselves against the sides, as they tried to protect Link, who suddenly became conscious and screamed in pain.

Rollo clasped a hand over his mouth, and Anna bent down to whisper in his ear. The sergeant swore in the front seat, and they all waited as the lights bore down on them, drew level and passed—it was an army truck full of troops.

They all sighed with relief when the sergeant started the engine again, and carefully edged their truck towards the road. But this time, it refused to mount the bank and they quickly became bogged down in the mud.

"All out and push," snarled the sergeant.

The engine roared as they all pushed and floundered in the growing mud hole. Finally, with an extra burst of engine power, the truck was over the bank, leaving everyone on their knees in the mud. Brett lifted the canvas flap and barked impatiently: "Get a move on."

The truck sped along the highway. The sergeant and Jake peered ahead into the darkness, and rounding a bend, Jake suddenly growled, "Pull over, Sarge, there's a barricade ahead. We'll walk from here, you turn and go back to camp.

Many thanks to you all, and safe journey."

"Same to you, Sir. Sure you can find your way?"

"We'll manage. Come on, family."

"I can't leave Link."

"For crying out loud, Anna, get out. He'll be fine if you let them go now, rather than later."

"But, Dad."

Meg gave Anna a gentle push, "Come on, love," she whispered, "we have to go."

Brett gave Anna's arm a squeeze, "He'll be okay, Anna. I promise."

Anna bent forward and gave Link a last kiss. She blindly clambered out of the truck after her mother and brother.

They stood watching, as the truck turned and sped back the way they'd come. Anna stood in the middle of the road, tears falling unheeded down her cheeks. Harry gave her a nudge, and her father growled, "Come on." Meg took her arm, and they followed Jake and Harry into the nearby field.

They stood silently, while Jake took his bearings and then, one behind the other, followed him as they crept around the sleeping village to avoid a roadblock.

At the river rendezvous it was very quiet and there was no boat in sight.

"Are you sure this is the place?"

"Yes, of course. You all stay here, I'm going to prowl around," and Jake slipped away up the bank.

Meg, Anna and Harry sat down wearily amongst the tall grasses. All their thoughts were on the marines and especially Link. Anna sighed softly, her tears all spent. Would she ever see him again?

Dawn was approaching, the air was starting to hum with bird and insect noises, and then Jake was there with a thin old man, who bobbed and grinned with terror and indicated, with a trembling hand, where his boat was hidden in the long grass.

They all helped to carry it down to the water as the sky became lighter every moment. Wading out into the water, Meg and Anna climbed in first, while Jake and Harry held the boat steady. The old man came scurrying down to the water with two rough paddles, and exchanged them with Jake for a bundle of notes, which he stuffed into the front of his shirt. Then he held the rocking boat steady by its side, while Jake and Harry pulled themselves into it.

For a long while, the man stood knee deep in the water watching them paddle away, then he turned and waded back to shore.

"What a sad farewell," said Meg, in a low voice. They were now midstream. For a moment they paused to gaze back at the deserted Lao shore as a new day dawned over the ancient kingdom of Lan Xang, the Land of a Million Elephants.

33

A Letter from Harry to His Friend Nat

Hi Nat:

. . . well that's what happened to us after you left. It was pretty sickening that we had to leave too, but we're spending time at the beach in Pattaya.

It was just amazing when these huge black-faced men came bursting into the classroom in the middle of the night. We didn't even have time to think who they were, we just knew they'd come to rescue us. Pretty cool, huh, being rescued by marines?

And what a scene met our eyes when we got outside. It was a real battle—guns, fires and guys being killed all over the place. It all seems like a replay of a movie or a nightmare now. . .

And would you believe it, Anna has fallen in love with one of the marines? It's pretty sickening really but, I suppose if she has to do something like that, a marine is a pretty good choice. They're okay guys. She was really upset having to leave him, but we soon heard that he was doing okay and was shipped out to the American base at Udon. In a couple of weeks, he's coming down to join us at the beach.

Mum and Dad are really great. They say there's no rush to go on anywhere, so we're spending our summer vacation here.

John came down to debrief us all—even me and Anna. He was mad to have missed all the fun. He'd fixed up jobs for Lian and Tee, and will keep in touch with them when he goes back for visits. Then he'll let us know how they're doing. Lian and her girls were very happy as they had seen Vang. He'd taken part in the raid, but he had to return to the mountains.

Mum is really upset that we had to leave Laos—we all are. It's a great place. Still there are lots of other places in the world to see, so we'll move on. It would be great if we end up in the same place as your family. Do you know where your dad's being posted? Of course, Dad will have to go and be briefed for his next job, but he's told them to leave him alone for six weeks. Way to go, Dad.

Mum says she doesn't mind where we go, but she has one condition: we have to go via Paris to visit Louis, Mimi, Guy, Pierre and Mr Lee. They're all having a good vacation in Paris after their terrible ordeals, before going on to Canada. Louis already has a job lined up, but the only deadline they have is to be settled before school starts.

We all agree with Mum about Paris. I'd love to climb the Eiffel Tower, and Dad wants to see those long-legged girls dancing the can-can!

Anna doesn't even want to think about the future. She's just counting the minutes till Link arrives here. Actually, Anna's a great sister, I'm kind of proud of her. But I still wish I'd been the one to escape. I must really be on my toes next time.

Well, I guess that's it. So long.

Harry Porter
from a Cottage on the Beach
Pattaya, Thailand
The Golden Triangle
South East Asia
The World
The Universe

PS. John brought Beauty and the cats to the beach. Beauty loves the water but the cats complain a lot. Mum says they'll be happier once we drop them off in Paris. Of course, Mimi may have to leave them there, 'cause I'm sure they'll really hate the snow.

H P

GLOSSARY

CIA: Central Intelligence Agency (American)
felang: foreigner (Lao)
HE: His Excellency (the Ambassador)
kip: Lao currency
Pathet Lao: meaning "Lao Country" in Lao—the name given to the Communist forces
samlow: tricycle with a rear seat for two
top: name given to marine sergeants
Udon: large town in Thailand within a few hours' drive from Vientiane
USAID: United States Agency for International Development
wat: Buddhist temple
yeun keun: get up (Lao)